A Dog's Heart

A Dog's Heart

A Monstrous Story

Mikhail Bulgakov

Translated by Hugh Aplin

Published by Hesperus Press Limited
28 Mortimer Street, London W1W 7RD
www.hesperuspress.com

A Dog's Heart first published in Russian in 1968
First published by Hesperus Press Limited, 2005
This edition printed 2012

Introduction and English language translation © Hugh Aplin, 2005
Foreword © A.S. Byatt, 2005

Designed and typeset by Fraser Muggeridge

ISBN: 978-1-84391-402-0

Contents

Foreword

A Dog's Heart was written between January and March 1925. Bulgakov read it to a gathering of forty-five people that March. A listener said, 'This is the first literary work that dares to be itself.' There was a project to publish it in the almanac *The Depths*, but on 7th May Bulgakov's flat was searched, and a typescript of the story was confiscated, with Bulgakov's diaries. This was the beginning of the censorship's opposition to Bulgakov, and the suppression of his writings which provoked his manifesto letter (published abroad) to the Soviet government dated 28th March 1930. In this letter he asks to be allowed to leave the country since his work is excoriated and its publication is prevented. The letter led to a phone call from Stalin himself, which resulted in work in the Moscow Art Theatre. But *A Dog's Heart* remained unpublished until it appeared in Germany in 1968. It appeared in Russia in 1987.

The tale was written during the relatively open time of Lenin's New Economic Policy (N.E.P.) when private economic activities offered Russians some autonomy as publishers or householders. Its author had already published a feuilleton, *A Treatise on Housing,* which consisted of semi-autobiographical accounts of the housing crisis. A recurrent theme in Bulgakov's work, from the early journalism to *The Master and Margarita,* is the chaos of housing communes and the lack of private space, so necessary to writers. Philipp Philippovich Preobrazhensky in this tale ferociously defends his living space by appealing to the influential people whom he is treating with his new methods of rejuvenation. This too was topical and real. Collections of articles, *Rejuvenation,* about organ transplants, were published in Russia in 1923 and 1924, claiming a successful transfer of organs from animals to men.

Bulgakov himself had given up a career as a doctor to become a writer. His uncle, N.M. Pokrovsky, was a Moscow gynaecologist who had had his living space drastically reduced, despite protests. *A Dog's Heart* is a fantasy embedded in precise reality. Even the wonderful spreads of caviar, veal, sturgeon, wines, rich sauces and vodka are things that were possible, briefly, during the N.E.P.

The brilliance of *A Dog's Heart* is in the energy and precision with which its world is made up. Talking dogs are not uncommon in literature. There is a letter-writing lapdog in Gogol's *Notes of a Madman*, who, as the insane narrator says, observes everything. 'Dogs are a clever lot, they know all the political relations, and so everything ought to be there: a picture of this man and all his doings...' Dogs are close to humans, and humans characteristically confer personality on them, and partly treat them as persons. One of the strokes of genius in Bulgakov's tale is the establishment of the dog-as-dog, *before his operation and humanisation*, as the most sympathetic character present. He suffers and is resourceful; he sympathises with the frozen typist whose lover only buys her silk stockings and flimsy lace panties; he has taught himself to read (backwards, we later discover, when he is learning real human speech). The professor, who is kind, tames him as a dog, before giving him human glands. Like the dog in Aesop's fable of the wolf and the dog, Sharik submits to a collar and comes to see it as the canine equivalent of a briefcase, a sign of status.

After he is operated on, he is seen from the outside, as a daemonic force for disorder. Terry Pratchett once said that his talking dog, Gaspode, was inspired by Sharik. Possibly he also took something from Sharik in his human form as Polygraph Polygraphovich for his cat-into-human, Greebo, and his werewolves teetering uneasily, ambimorphic, between the human and the canine. Bulgakov's dog-man is degenerate and disgusting, as dog and man, interested in fleas, cats, political denunciation and rape.

When *A Dog's Heart* was first available, both in the West and in the Soviet Union of glasnost, it was seen as a satire on Soviet society. Sharikov and the narrow-minded petty members of the House Committee, with whom as a man he associates himself, are creatures unnaturally taken out of their proper setting and given power. Sharik in dog form approves of the professor's routing of this committee, comparing the professor to a dog. ' "This lad here," thought the dog in delight, "is just like me. Ooh, he'll take a bite out of them in a minute, ooh, he'll take a bite. I don't know in what way yet, but he'll take such a bite... Give them one! Grab that lanky one a little way above his boot by the tendon at the back of the knee..." ' Some readers have supposed that Bulgakov sympathises with – identifies with – his irascible professor, but I don't think that the feeling of the story justifies this idea.

Like Professor Persikov, in *The Fatal Eggs,* Philipp Philippovich is both a man of science and a sorcerer, conjuring new and dangerous forms of life into being, and then losing control of them. He is scornful of the disorder brought about by the sudden changes introduced by the Revolution and what his assistant, Dr Bormental, refers to as 'the collapse', which is both the malfunction of things like heating and plumbing, and something resembling the hectic chaos of a witches' sabbath. In *The Fatal Eggs*, the state breeds monsters from eggs, with the aid of a 'red ray', and the monsters wreak havoc and destroy communities. Philipp Philippovich makes a dog-man, and this creature destroys his comfortable environment much more thoroughly than the House Committee manages to do. The episode of the dog-man being locked in the lavatory, having pursued a tomcat there, and flooding the house, is totally chaotic and wildly funny. If 'the collapse' is a name for social disorder, Bulgakov's art of depicting chaos derives from the great phantasmagoria of Goethe's 'Brocken scene', Hoffmann's eerie tales and Gogol's witches and animated body-parts. *The Fatal Eggs* was published in a collection called *Diaboliad*. The two professors are precursors of the urbane conjurer-demon, Woland, of *The Master and Margarita*.

In his letter to the Soviet government Bulgakov claims to be a *'mystic writer'* whose satire is not meant to lampoon the Revolution. ('It is *impossible* to write a lampoon on an event of such extreme grandeur as the Revolution.') He rejects his critics' automatic assumption that *'any satirist in the USSR is attacking the Soviet system.'* Nevertheless he asserts that he feels 'deep scepticism with regard to the revolutionary process taking place in my backward country and counterposed to it... love for Great Evolution.'

Philipp Philippovich, renouncing his revolutionary experiment, points out ruefully and vehemently that there is no need to implant Spinoza's pituitary gland into a dog to make a being of a high order. 'Explain to me, please, why one needs to fabricate Spinozas artificially, when a woman can give birth to him any time you like.' He goes on to say that Mme Lomonosova produced her famous offspring in just that way. Lomonosov was an eighteenth-century polymath and academician, son of a poor fisherman. Workers become great men by evolution, not revolution.

A Dog's Heart is more than a satire – it is a sharp and complicated moral fable, funny and profound, by one of the great writers of the twentieth century.

– A.S. Byatt, 2005

Introduction

In the early 1920s there was a great deal of interest both within post-revolutionary Russia and abroad in the possibility of rejuvenating living organisms. Mikhail Bulgakov, as a trained doctor and a practising journalist, could not help but become familiar with the articles, some scientific, some of a more popular nature, that appeared in considerable numbers in a range of Russian publications of the day. At Moscow's Colossus cinema in 1923 it was even possible to see a documentary film about the Austrian physiologist Eugen Steinach's work on the problem, and an advertisement for this screening may have inspired the poster that poses the question in the opening pages of *A Dog's Heart*: 'Is rejuvenation possible?' The confident reply of the dog that reads the question is 'of course', but that response reflects the immediate rejuvenating effect on a doomed creature's instinct for survival when confronted with the appearance of hope. As subsequent decades were to demonstrate, far less certain is the possibility of significant scientific progress in allowing human beings to stay younger longer; and hardly less problematic was the achievement of a rejuvenated society in the conditions of Soviet Russia.

However, the dog's chance encounter with the bearer of hope, Professor Preobrazhensky, while presenting it with the unexpected opportunity to be itself rejuvenated by a successful specialist in precisely that field, actually precipitates a much more drastic change for the unfortunate animal. Had it been more experienced in linguistic matters, the dog might have understood that the professor's very name portends not mere rejuvenation, but complete 'transfiguration' (*preobrazheniye*). The dog's obliviousness is, of course, understandable, all the more since even the scientist himself is unaware, when planning and performing the operation that turns dog into man, of what the outcome will be. The operation is a mistake in two ways: firstly, it brings about a result that was unintended and unforeseen, and secondly – and ultimately more importantly – a result that is unacceptable to its perpetrator: namely, the creation of the new man, Sharikov.

The 'new man', like 'rejuvenation', was a concept much in vogue in Soviet Russia. The new man, forged in the fires of revolution and civil war, was to be instrumental in creating a new society, at first Socialist, then finally Communist. Yet the 'homo socialisticus' of which the philosopher Sergei Bulgakov was writing disparagingly as early as 1918, developed all too readily into the 'homo sovieticus', satirised and condemned by Alexander Zinoviev in 1981, shortly before the type's demise. Sharikov soon falls in with the enthusiastic but unimaginative and limited activists who aim to educate him in Socialist dogma and social responsibility and thus make him a positive contributor to the creation of a bright Soviet future. The futility of this brave intention rapidly becomes clear, first and foremost to Preobrazhensky. His conviction is that the raw material from which he has unwittingly created a new man is unpropitious – and that the deficiency is not the fault of the dog's heart that contributes to the creature that is Sharikov. The dog's instincts for sustenance and shelter, shared by Klim Chugunkin, the donor of the crucial pituitary gland, are seen to be natural and unexceptionable; but the dog's gratitude and loyalty to his benefactor are not shared by the Chugunkin-controlled Sharikov. His allegiances are patently limited to his own self. And where the dog was responsive to education, even adopting elements of the professor's speech patterns, Sharikov proves to be a cultural force capable of rivalling his would-be mentors: the cheap balalaika music he has inherited from Chugunkin ousts grand opera from Preobrazhensky's head, and money taken from the Bolsheviks ostensibly for books is squandered on vodka (wine he dislikes), women and song. His lying, thieving and vindictiveness mean that not only is Sharikov less attractive than the dog that preceded him: he is by far the moral inferior of even that not-so-dumb animal.

Indeed, the morality of men in general is called into question in this work, from the very first page onwards. The behaviour of most of those observed by the dog is deemed by him reprehensible, from the embezzling bureaucrat to the adulterous libertine, and most obvious of all is the cruelty of the cook in the dirty cap. Preobrazhensky seems to represent a different branch of humanity with his kindness to animals, civility to subordinates and adherence to pre-revolutionary cultural values. Yet the very nature of his experiments, particularly given the manner in which the pivotal operation is described, cannot be passed over lightly; the high priest of science is shown to be harsh and bestial, and the cap he is mentioned as wearing both during the transplant operation and later on, when he acts to undo his error, implicitly links him with the cap that represents the heartless cook. In these days of stern defence of the rights of animals, many might join the dog in questioning what it had done to deserve its treatment. No less problematic is the fate of Sharikov. Odious as he clearly is, he nonetheless surely has undeniable rights as a human being – albeit one of strange and mixed origins – yet the professor and his assistant behave towards him from an early stage in a way that suggests they are scarcely prepared to acknowledge his status. One cannot help but reflect on the justice or otherwise of their attitudes, and this must have a negative impact on the reader's assessment of the professor and the values for which he stands. Even the grasping of moral responsibility that leads to the story's conclusion is fraught with ethical difficulties, given the means used to implement that responsibility.

Much of Preobrazhensky's privileged position within the narrative stems from the initial canine point of view. As the dog's benefactor, provider of food, warmth and security, the professor is instantly lionised and very soon deified. His discourteous dismissal of the House Committee, which might otherwise seem unnecessarily brusque – if only in his refusal to make a charitable purchase – is recorded with unbounded admiration by the terroriser of cats and timid humans. Unsurprisingly, the dog is prepared to accept punishment and adopt a position of subservience in the face of benign authority (or enlightened despotism). However, the passing of the dog's perspective diminishes Preobrazhensky quite considerably. His assistant's admiration compensates to some extent for the loss of the dog's, but the doctor's conduct of the narrative is but brief, and the largely dramatic nature of the third-person narration thereafter reveals Preobrazhensky battling far less successfully than previously, not only against the House Committee, but also against that other would-be invader of his personal living space, Sharikov. It is ironic that the home he defends so stoutly against the attempted incursions of the House Committee is infiltrated so easily by the fruit of the research that actually allows him that space. He is demonstrably weakened by the presence of the interloper, and yet it is arguably Sharikov's unattractive behaviour, his intrusion into and destruction of the haven that had been so valued by the homeless dog, that ensures, more than any occupation of moral high ground, the reader's continuing sympathy for the irritable and increasingly uncertain professor.

Preobrazhensky's response to the consequences of the fall of the Romanov dynasty is exclusively negative, and often violently so, but his attitude is not necessarily at odds with his generally humane nature. For his objections appear to be based not so much on the essence of revolutionary principles as on their adaptation to actual circumstances and the crudeness of the new authorities' attempts to impose their new social order. The democratic principle was, after all, one espoused by the majority of Russia's intelligentsia, who played a crucial role in the preparation for the overthrow of the autocracy. But the ineptitude of Russia's new rulers and the vulgar egalitarianism of the desire to 'share everything out' fill Preobrazhensky with horror, as he sees the world he inhabits threatened by philistinism and potential chaos. The House Committee represents some of the failings of the regime, while Sharikov is a vivid incarnation of the monster that, between them, the old Russian intelligentsia and the new Russian ideologues have contrived to create. Preobrazhensky regards the resurrected Chugunkin as irredeemable, and it is difficult for the reader not to concur: the new man whose initial development occurs ironically between the dates of the Western and Orthodox Christmases is, as his almost blasphemous choice of name testifies, more a devilish figure than a Socialist Messiah. Characteristics acceptable in a dog, one must conclude, are quite inadmissible in a man.

– Hugh Aplin, 2005

Note on the Text:

A Dog's Heart was intended to be published in the almanac *The Depths* soon after its completion in March 1925, but it fell foul of the censor and this plan could not be realised. Attempts were made to render the text more acceptable by editing, and an amended copy was even sent – without success – to L.B. Kamenev, at that time a leading member of the government. The story was, nonetheless, already familiar to many from the author's readings, and various copies of the text soon entered into circulation through the phenomenon of *samizdat*. The result of all this was that there was no definitive version of the text authorised during the writer's lifetime for adoption by posterity. The first publications of Russian texts of *A Dog's Heart* were in Frankfurt, London and Paris in 1968 and 1969, but the work appeared in the Soviet Union only in 1987. Since that time the work has been republished regularly in Russia, both in collections of Bulgakov's writing, and in separate editions, with numerous variations, mostly small, but sometimes more significant. The basic text used for this translation is that found in volume two of a five-volume collection published in Moscow by *Khudozhestvennaya literatura* in 1991. However, a number of other editions have been consulted and, where possible, fragments of text which appear elsewhere but not in this 1991 edition have been included in the translation with the aim of allowing the reader the fullest possible impression of Bulgakov's work. Where textual variants were found to be mutually exclusive, the 1991 text was the one preferred.

A Dog's Heart

Ow-ow-ow-ow-ow – bow-wow-wo-ow! Oh, look at me, I'm done for. The blizzard in the gateway is wailing out a prayer for the dying to me, and I'm howling along with it. It's all over for me, over. A wretch in a dirty cap – a cook in the standard food canteen for office staff from the Central Soviet of the People's Economy – has poured boiling water over me and scalded my left side. What a bastard – and a proletarian too. Oh Lord God – how it hurts! Eaten through to the bone with boiling water. Now I'm howling and howling, but what good will howling do?

What had I done to him? Am I really going to clean out the Soviet of the People's Economy by digging around in a rubbish heap? The greedy beast! Just you take a look sometime at his ugly mug: he's wider than he's tall, you know. A thief with a brassy face. Ah, people, people. At midday cap man treated me to the boiling water, and now it's got dark, it's about four in the afternoon, judging by the smell of onions from the Prechistenka fire brigade. Firemen have porridge for dinner, as you're aware. But this is the worst thing there is, rather like mushrooms. Incidentally, some dogs I know from Prechistenka were saying that in The Bar restaurant on Neglinny people guzzle the *plat du jour* – mushrooms with a piquant sauce – at three roubles seventy-five kopeks a portion. That's something you need to have a taste for – you might as well be licking a galosh... Ow-ow-ow-ow-ow...

My side's unbearably painful, and I can see the far end of my career quite distinctly: tomorrow ulcers will appear and what, one might ask, am I going to use to treat them? In the summer you can nip up to Sokolniki[1], there's a very good special sort of grass there, and apart from that you can stuff yourself for free on the ends of sticks of salami, and the citizens throw loads of greasy paper around, you can have a good lick of that. And if it weren't for some caterwauler that sings in a ring in the moonlight – 'sweet Aïda'[2] – in a way that makes your heart sink, it would be great. But where can you go now? Have you been kicked up the backside by a boot? You have. Have you had a brick in the ribs? You've had your fill of it. I've experienced everything, I'm becoming reconciled to my fate, and if I'm crying now, it's only from the physical pain and hunger, because my spirit hasn't failed yet... A dog's spirit hangs on to life.

But my body, now, it's broken, beaten, people have ill-treated it enough. And you know, the main thing is the way he laid into me with the boiling water, it ate in under the coat, and so there's no protection whatsoever for my left side. I might very easily catch pneumonia, and if I get that, citizens, I'll drop dead of hunger. With pneumonia you're supposed to lie and rest under a front entrance stairway, but then who's going to run around the rubbish bins in search of food instead of me, a resting bachelor dog? It'll get into my lung, I'll start crawling on my belly, get weaker, and any old dogcatcher'll beat me to death with a stick. And janitors with metal badges'll grab me by the legs and chuck me out onto a cart...

Of all proletarians, janitors are the vilest scum. Human peelings – the lowest category. You come across a variety of cooks. The late Vlas from Prechistenka, for example. How many lives did he save? Because the main thing during an illness is snatching a bite to eat. And sometimes, so the old dogs say, Vlas would fling a bone out and there'd be a couple of ounces of meat left on it. May he rest in peace for being a genuine character, family cook to the Counts Tolstoy, and not from the Soviet of Standard Food. What they get up to there in Standard Food is beyond the comprehension of a dog's mind. I mean, the scoundrels, they make cabbage soup using reeking salted meat, and the other ones, the poor things, don't even know a thing. They come running, stuff it down, lap it up.

Some nice little typist gets forty-five roubles in grade IX, well, true, her lover'll give her *fil de Perse*[3] stockings. But I mean, how many insults does she have to bear in return for that *fil de Perse*? I mean, he doesn't give it her in some ordinary way, but rather subjects her to French love. Swine they are, those Frenchmen, between you and me. Even if they do eat well, and always with red wine. Yes... The typist'll come running, I mean, you can't go to The Bar on forty-five roubles. She doesn't even have enough to go to the cinematograph; and the cinematograph's a woman's only consolation in life. She shudders, she grimaces, but she eats... Just think: forty kopeks for two courses, but the two of those courses aren't together worth even fifteen kopeks, because the remaining twenty-five kopeks have been stolen by the finance manager. And does she really need cooking like that? The upper part of her right lungs's not in order, and she's got a lady's disease because of the French business, they've deducted money from her at work, they've fed her tainted meat in the canteen, and here she is, here she is... She's running through the gateway in her lover's stockings. Her legs are cold, the wind's blowing right into her stomach, because the coat on her's like mine, but she wears thin knickers; just a lacy semblance alone. Rags for the lover. Let her try putting on flannel ones and he'll start yelling: how inelegant you are! I'm fed up with my Matryona, flannel knickers have worn me out, and now my time has come. I'm the chairman now, and no matter how much I steal – it all goes on the female body, on Crayfish Necks, on Abrau Durso.[4] Because I went hungry quite enough in my youth, that's your lot from me, and the afterlife doesn't exist.

I'm sorry for her, so sorry! But I'm even more sorry for myself. I'm not speaking out of egotism, oh no, but because we really aren't on equal terms. At least she's warm at home, but what about me, what about me... Where can I go? Beaten, scalded, spat upon, wherever can I go? Ow-ow-ow-ow-ow!...

'Come on, come on, come on! Sharik, hey, Sharik... What are you howling about, you poor thing? Who's hurt you? Ooh...'

The dry witch of the snowstorm crashed the gates about and rode on its broomstick over the young lady's ear. It whipped her flimsy skirt up around her knees, bared her cream stockings and the narrow strip of poorly laundered lace underwear, stifled the words and covered the dog in snow.

'My God... What weather... Ooh... And I've got a stomach-ache. It's the salted meat, it's the salted meat. And when will all this ever end?'

Bending her head down, the young lady rushed onto the attack, burst through the gates, and out in the street she was spun around, spun around, torn apart, tossed about, then she was screwed up tight into a screw of snow and disappeared.

But the dog remained in the gateway and, suffering from its injured side, pressed up against the cold wall, gasped for breath and firmly resolved that it would never again go anywhere away from here, and here in the gateway it would die. Despair had toppled it. It felt so hurt and bitter in its soul, so lonely and afraid, that little canine tears crawled out of its eyes like little bumps and dried up on the spot. Tangled frozen lumps stuck out from its damaged side, and from between them gazed the red, ominous marks of the scalding. How senseless, stupid and cruel cooks are. 'Sharik,' she had called him... What kind of 'Sharik' was he, damn it? 'Sharik' means round, well fed, stupid, eats oat porridge, the son of exalted parents, whereas he is shaggy, lanky and ragged, a wiry tramp, a homeless mutt. But thanks for the kind word anyway.

Across the street the door slammed in a brightly lit shop, and from it there appeared a citizen. Specifically a citizen and not a comrade, and even – most precisely of all – a gentleman. The closer, the clearer – a gentleman. You think I'm judging by his overcoat? Nonsense. Overcoats are worn by very large numbers nowadays, even among the proletarians. It's true, the collars aren't so good, there's no argument about that, but all the same, you can confuse them from a distance. But going by the eyes – now there you won't confuse them either close up or from a distance. Oh, eyes are a significant thing. Like a barometer. Everything's visible – who's got a great drought in their soul, who without rhyme or reason can jab the toe of their boot into your ribs, and who's scared of everything themselves. And it's precisely this latter lackey that it's sometimes nice to grab by the ankle-bone. You're scared – then take that. If you're scared, that means you deserve it... r-r-r... woof-woof...

The gentleman confidently cut across the street in the very thick of the snowstorm and moved into the gateway. Yes indeed, this one has everything on show. This one wouldn't think of guzzling rotten salted meat, and if he were to be served it anywhere, he'd make such a fuss – write to the newspapers: 'I, Philipp Philippovich, have been poisoned'.

Now he's ever closer and closer. This one eats plentifully and doesn't steal, this one won't think of kicking you, but he's not scared of anyone himself either, and he's not scared because he's permanently full. He's a gentleman of intellectual labour with a sharply pointed little French beard and grey whiskers, fluffy and dashing like French knights have, but the scent that flies from him through the snowstorm is nasty – it's of a hospital. And a cigar.

What the devil, one might ask, has brought him to the Central Soviet of the People's Economy cooperative? Here he is, right alongside... What's he trying to find? Ow-ow-ow-ow... What could he have been buying in that lousy little shop – isn't Okhotny Row[5] enough for him? What's that? Sa-la-mi. Mister, if you saw what they make that salami out of, you wouldn't go anywhere near the shop. Give it to me.

The dog collected what was left of its strength and crawled in a frenzy out of the gateway onto the pavement. The blizzard gave a shot from a gun overhead, flung up the huge letters of a linen poster: 'Is rejuvenation possible?'

Naturally it's possible. A scent's rejuvenated me, got me up off my belly, its burning waves have cramped a stomach empty for two whole days, a scent that's overcome the hospital, a heavenly scent of minced mare with garlic and pepper. I sense, I know – he has salami in the right-hand pocket of his fur coat. He's above me. O my lord! Look at me. I'm dying. Our servile soul, our ignoble lot!

In floods of tears the dog began crawling on its belly like a snake. Pay attention to the work of the cook. But you won't give it, will you, not for anything. Oh, I know rich people so well! But what do you want it for, essentially? What do you want mouldy horsemeat for? You'll get muck like that nowhere but from Mosselprom.[6] And you've had your breakfast today, you great man of global significance thanks to the male sex glands. Ow-ow-ow-ow... What ever is going on in this world? It's evidently early yet to be dying – and despair... that really is a sin. Lick his hands, there's nothing else for it.

The mysterious gentleman bent down to the dog, flashed the gold rims of his eyes and drew from his right-hand pocket a white oblong package. Without removing his brown gloves, he unwound the paper, of which the snowstorm immediately took possession, and broke off a piece of salami called 'Cracow Special'. And this piece went to the dog. O unselfish individual! Ow-ow-ow!

'Hey boy, hey boy,' called the gentleman, and added in a stern voice: 'Take it! Sharik, Sharik!'

Again 'Sharik'. Christened. Whatever name you like. In return for your deed, so exceptional.

The dog instantly ripped off the skin, sank its teeth into the Cracow with a sob and scoffed it down in a trice. In doing so it choked on the salami and snow to the point of tears, because in its greed it had all but swallowed the string. I lick your hand again and again. I kiss your trousers, my benefactor!

'Enough for now…' The gentleman spoke thus, abruptly, as though giving commands. He bent down to Sharik, gave him a searching look in the eyes and unexpectedly passed the hand in the glove intimately and tenderly over Sharik's stomach.

'Aha,' he said meaningfully, 'no collar… well, that's splendid, you're the one that I'm looking for, then. Follow me.' He clicked his fingers. 'Come on, come on!'

Follow you? To the ends of the earth. Kick me in the face with your felt boots, I won't say a word.

The streetlights were shining all down Prechistenka. His side was unbearably painful, but Sharik forgot it at times, absorbed by the one thought – not to lose in the commotion the wonderful vision in the fur coat, and somehow to express to him his love and devotion. And some seven times over the length of Prechistenka as far as Obukhov Lane he did express it. He kissed his shoe; by Myortvy Lane, in clearing the way, he so frightened some lady with his wild howling that she sat down on a kerbside post; a couple of times he whimpered to maintain feelings of pity for him.

Some scummy tramp of a tomcat made to look like a Siberian dived out from behind a drainpipe and, despite the blizzard, it sniffed out the Cracow. Sharik went wild with rage at the thought that the wealthy crank who picks up wounded dogs in gateways might well take this thief along with him, and he would have to share the product of Mosselprom. And so he rattled his teeth at the cat in such a way that the latter, with a hissing like the hissing of a hose full of holes, climbed up a drainpipe to the first floor. – F-r-r-r... woof! Be off! There'll never be enough from Mosselprom for all the various bits of trash drifting up and down Prechistenka.

The gentleman showed his appreciation of the devotion, and right by the fire station, by a window from which could be heard the pleasant grumbling of a French horn, he rewarded the dog with a second morsel, a little smaller, about twenty grams.

Hah, the crank. Drawing me on. Don't worry! I won't be going off anywhere by myself. I'll be moving along behind you, wherever you want me to.

'Come on, come on, come on! This way!'

Into Obukhov? If you please. We're very familiar with this lane.

'Come on, come on!'

This way? With pleasu... Ah, no! Permit me. No! There's a doorman here. And there's absolutely nothing on earth worse than that. Many times more dangerous than a janitor. An utterly hateful breed. Fouler than tomcats. A dog-killer in braid.

'Don't be afraid now, come on.'

'Good day to you, Philipp Philippovich.'

'Hello, Fyodor.'

Now that's a personality. My God, whoever have you bumped me up against, O my canine lot! What sort of person is this that can take dogs from the street past doormen into the building of a housing association? Look, that bastard – not a sound, not a movement! True, his eyes are sullen, but on the whole he's indifferent underneath the cap-band with gold galloons. As though this is the way it should be. Respectful he is, gentlemen, how very respectful! Well, sir, I'm with him and following him. What, did he touch you? Bite. I'd love to have a chunk of his calloused proletarian leg. In return for all the insults from your kind. How many times have you scarred my face with brushes, eh?

'Come on, come on.'

We understand, we understand, there's no need to worry. Wherever you go, I'll be there too. You just show me the way, and I won't lag behind in spite of my desperate flank.

From the staircase to below:

'Were there no letters for me, Fyodor?'

Up the staircase from below, deferentially:

'No, Philipp Philippovich,' (intimately, in a low voice in pursuit) 'but some house-comrades have been moved into apartment number three.'

The grand canine philanthropist turned around sharply on the step and, bending over the banister, he asked in horror:

'What's that?'

His eyes had grown rounded and his whiskers stood on end.

From below the doorman tilted his head back, put the palm of his hand to his lips and confirmed:

'Yes, sir, a whole four of them.'

'My God! I can just imagine what will happen in the apartment now. Well, and what did they do?'

'Nothing much, sir.'

'And Fyodor Pavlovich?'

'Gone to get screens and bricks. He's going to put up partitions.'

'The devil knows what's going on!'

'People are going to be moved into all the apartments, Philipp Philippovich, except for yours. There's just been a meeting, a new association's been elected, and the previous one's got it in the neck.'

'The things that go on. Dear-oh-dear… Come on, come on.'

Coming, sir, making haste. The side, you see, is making itself felt. Allow me to give your boot a lick.

Downstairs the doorman's galloon disappeared. On the marble landing warmth was wafting from the pipes, they took another turn and there it was – the *bel étage*.

2

There's absolutely no point learning to read when you can smell meat a kilometre away as it is. Nevertheless, if you're resident in Moscow and you've got any brains in your head at all, willy-nilly you'll become literate, and, what's more, without any kind of classes. Out of forty thousand Muscovite dogs it could only be some complete idiot that wouldn't know how to put together the letters of the word 'salami'.

Sharik began learning by colours. He was only just four months old when across the whole of Moscow they hung out greenish-blue signs with the inscription 'M.U.C.S.[7] Meat trading'. We repeat, all this is pointless, because meat can be smelt as it is. And one time Sharik got into a muddle: going by the acidic bluish colour, and with his sense of smell battered by the petrol fumes from a motor, rather than at a butcher's he rolled up at the electrical accessories shop of Golubizner Bros. on Myasnitskaya Street.[8] There at the brothers' place the dog got a taste of insulation wire, and that's rather sharper than a cabman's whip. It's this celebrated moment that should be considered the start of Sharik's education. Right there on the pavement Sharik already began to realise that 'blue' did not always signify 'meat', and, with his tail pressed between his hind legs at the burning pain and howling, he recalled that first on the left on all the butchers' shops was a gold or ginger bow-legged thing that looked like a sleigh.

Later on, things went even more successfully. 'H' he learnt in State Fish on the corner of Mokhovaya, and then 'S' too – it was easier for him to come running up from the tail of the word 'Fish', because at the beginning of the word there stood a policeman.

The little square tiles that covered the surfaces of the places on corners in Moscow always and inevitably signified 'C-h-e-e-s-e'.

The black handle that headed the word designated the former owner, Chichkin[9], mountains of Dutch red, brutes of shop assistants who hated dogs, sawdust on the floor and the most foul, evil-smelling Limburg.

If there was an accordion being played, which was little better than 'sweet Aïda', and there was a smell of sausages, the first letters on the white posters formed extremely neatly into the word 'indece...', which signified 'indecent language forbidden and no tips'. Here from time to time fights boiled over and spiralled, and people were punched in the face – in rare instances, true – while dogs were hit continually – by napkins or boots.

If there were stale hams hanging in the windows and mandarins lying about... grrr-grrr... gr... ocer's. If there were dark bottles with bad liquid... dubl-u-i – wi – en-e – wine... The Yeliseyevs[10], the former brothers.

The unknown gentleman who had drawn the dog to the doors of his luxury apartment situated on the *bel étage* rang the bell, and straight away the dog raised its eyes to the large black card with gold letters that hung to the side of the wide door, glazed with rippled and pink glass. It put the first three letters together straight away: 'Pe-ar-o – Pro'. But further on was some lanky, stooping rubbish, designating who knows what. 'Surely not proletarian?' thought Sharik in surprise... 'That can't be right.' He lifted his nose up, sniffed at the fur coat once more and thought confidently: 'No, there's no smell of proletarian here. A highbrow word, but God knows what it means.'

Behind the pink glass an unexpected and joyous light flared up and made the black card stand out all the more. The door swung open quite noiselessly and a pretty young woman in a little white apron and a lace cap appeared before the dog and his gentleman. A heavenly warmth washed over the former of them, and the woman's skirt gave off a smell like lily of the valley.

'Now this is really something. This I can appreciate,' thought the dog.

'Do please go in, Mr Sharik,' the gentleman invited him ironically, and Sharik did reverentially go in, wagging his tail.

A great multitude of objects crammed the rich entrance hall. Immediately memorable were a mirror reaching right down to the floor, which straight away reflected a second worn out and ragged Sharik, terrifying deer antlers way up high, innumerable fur coats and galoshes, and an opal tulip with electricity just below the ceiling.

'Where ever did you get a thing like that, Philipp Philippovich?' asked the woman with a smile, helping him take off his heavy fur coat of dark-red fox with a bluish shimmer. 'Heavens! How mangy he is!'

'You're talking nonsense. Where is he mangy?' asked the gentleman sternly and abruptly.

Upon the removal of the fur coat he turned out to be wearing a dark suit of English cloth, and on his stomach there glittered joyfully and sombrely a gold chain.

'Hang on, stop spinning round, hey... stop spinning round, will you, you stupid thing. Hm!... That's not mange... Just keep still, damn it... Hm! Ah-ah. That's a scald. What villain was it scalded you? Eh? Now just stand quietly!...'

'That crook of a cook... the cook!' said the dog's plaintive eyes, and he gave a little whimper.

'Zina,' commanded the gentleman, 'into the consulting room with him straight away, and bring me my coat.'

The woman whistled, clicked her fingers, and the dog, after a little hesitation, followed her. The two of them went into a narrow, dimly lit corridor, they passed one varnished door, arrived at the end, and then went to the left, and ended up in a dark boxroom to which, with its ominous smell, the dog took an instant dislike. The darkness clicked and turned into blinding day, at which on all sides there was a sudden flashing, a shining, a whiteness.

'Ah, no,' the dog began howling inside its head, 'I'm sorry, I won't give myself up! Oh, I understand, and to hell with them and their salami too. It's a dogs' clinic they've enticed me into. They'll make me swallow castor oil now, and cut my whole side to shreds with knives, although it can't even be touched at all!'

'Oh no, where are you going?!' cried the one who was called Zina.

The dog dodged, coiled up like a spring and suddenly banged his healthy side against the door such that the crash was heard all through the apartment. Then he flew backwards and began whirling around on the spot like a pegtop under a whip, and in so doing tipped over onto the floor a white bucket from which balls of cotton wool flew in all directions. During the spinning, all around him fluttered walls covered by cabinets full of shining instruments, and a white apron and a contorted female face began to jump.

'Where are you going, you shaggy-haired devil?...' cried Zina desperately, 'you damned thing!'

'Where's their back staircase?...' wondered the dog. He struck out and banged at random like a ball into glass, in the hope that it was a second door. A shower of splinters flew out with a thundering and a ringing, a rounded jar bounced out full of ginger muck which instantly flooded the whole floor and began to stink. The real door swung open.

'Stop, you b-beast,' cried the gentleman, jumping about with only one arm in the sleeve of a white coat and grabbing the dog by the legs. 'Zina, hold him by the scruff of the neck, the swine!'

'Hea... Heavens, now there's a dog!'

The door swung open yet wider, and yet another person of male gender wearing a white coat burst in. Trampling on the broken glass, it hurled itself not towards the dog, but to a cabinet, it opened it and filled the whole room with a sweet and sickening smell. Then the person fell upon the dog stomach-first from above, at which the dog bit it enthusiastically a little way above the laces on its shoe. The person gasped but wasn't shaken off. The nauseating liquid caught the dog's breath, and everything began spinning in his head, then his legs fell off and he started out crookedly off to one side somewhere. 'Thank you, it's over,' he thought dreamily, collapsing right onto the sharp bits of glass. 'Farewell, Moscow! I won't see Chichkin any more, or the proletarians, or Cracow salami. I'm going to Heaven for my canine long-suffering. My dog-killing chums, why did you do it to me?'

And here he collapsed completely onto his side and died.

* * *

When he rose again, his head was spinning slightly and he felt a little sick in his stomach, while it was as if his side weren't there, his side was sweetly silent. The dog opened his languid right eye a little and from its corner he saw that he was tightly bandaged across the sides and stomach. 'Stitched me up after all, the sons of bitches,' he thought confusedly, 'but skilfully, I've got to give them their due.'

'"From Seville unto Granada... In the soft dusk of the nights[11]",' a voice began to sing above him, absent-minded and out of tune.

The dog was surprised, opened both eyes completely and saw, two paces away from him, a man's leg on a white stool. The trouser leg and long johns it was wearing were pulled up, and the bare yellow shin was daubed with dried blood and iodine.

'Saints alive!' thought the dog. 'So then, it was him I bit. My work. Well, they'll give me a thrashing!'

'"There ring out sweet songs of ardour, There rings out the clash of fights!" Why did you bite the doctor, you tramp? Eh? What did you break the glass for? Eh?'

'Ow-ow-ow,' the dog began to whine plaintively.

'All right then, you've come round, so just lie there, halfwit.'

'Philipp Philippovich, how did you manage to entice such a nervy dog?' asked a pleasant male voice, and the tricot long johns rolled away downwards. There was a smell of tobacco, and phials clinked in a cabinet.

'With kindness, sir. The only method that's possible in dealing with a living creature. You can't do anything with an animal by terror, no matter what rung of development it stands on. I have asserted that, I do assert it and shall continue to assert it. They're wrong to think that terror will help them. No, sir, no, sir, it won't help, whichever it might be: white, red, even brown! Terror completely paralyses the nervous system. Zina! I bought this scoundrel one rouble forty kopek's worth of Cracow salami. Be so kind as to feed him when he stops being sick.'

Swept-up bits of glass crunched and a female voice remarked coquettishly:

'Cracow! Good Lord, you should have bought him twenty kopeks' worth of scraps at the butcher's. Better if I eat the Cracow salami myself.'

'Just you try. I'll give you "eat it"! It's poison for the human stomach. A grown-up girl, but just like a child, you put all sorts of muck in your mouth. Don't you dare! I warn you: neither I nor Dr Bormental will be fussing over you when you get stomach cramps... "All who tell me that another... bears comparison with you..."'

Soft, staccato little ringing sounds were sprinkling all through the apartment at this time, and in the distance from the entrance hall voices kept on being heard. The telephone was ringing. Zina disappeared.

Philipp Philippovich threw the stub of his cigarette into the bin, buttoned up his white coat, smoothed out his fluffy whiskers in front of the little mirror on the wall and called to the dog:

'Come on, come on. Well, it's all right, it's all right. Let's go and see some people.'

The dog rose onto unsteady legs, swayed a little and trembled a bit, but quickly recovered and set off after Philipp Philippovich's fluttering coat-tail. Again the dog crossed the narrow corridor, but now he saw it was brightly lit from above by a light fitting. And when the varnished door opened, he and Philipp Philippovich went into the study, and the latter blinded the dog with its decoration. First and foremost, the whole of it blazed with light: there was burning just below the moulded ceiling, there was burning on the table, there was burning on the wall, in the glass of the cabinets. Light flooded a whole host of objects, of which the most absorbing proved to be an immense owl, sitting on the wall on a bough.

'Lie down,' ordered Philipp Philippovich.

The carved door opposite opened, and in came the other one, the bitten one, who proved now in the bright light to be very handsome, young, with a sharp little beard; he handed over a sheet of paper and said:

'The one from before...'

He immediately disappeared without a sound, while Philipp Philippovich, spreading out the tails of his white coat, sat down at an immense desk and straight away became extraordinarily grand and imposing.

'No, this isn't a clinic, I've ended up in some other sort of place somewhere,' thought the dog in confusion, and lay himself down on the pattern of the carpet by a heavy leather couch, 'but we'll have to clear up the matter of that owl...'

The door opened softly, and in came someone who so astonished the dog, he let out a yap, but very timidly...

'Quiet! Bah, but you're quite unrecognisable, my dear fellow.'

The man who had come in bowed to Philipp Philippovich with great deference and embarrassment.

'Hee-hee! You are a magician and an enchanter, Professor,' he said, abashed.

'Take your trousers off, my dear fellow,' commanded Philipp Philippovich, and rose.

'Lord Jesus,' thought the dog, 'there's a fruit for you!'

On the fruit's head grew completely green hair, and at the back it was shot with a rusty tobacco colour, wrinkles were spreading all over the fruit's face, but his complexion was pink like a baby's. His left leg did not bend and had to be dragged across the carpet, whereas the right one leapt like one on a child's nutcracker. On the breast of a most magnificent jacket a precious stone stuck out like an eye.

The dog's interest even made his nausea pass.

'Yap, yap!' he yapped gently.

'Quiet! How are you sleeping, my dear fellow?'

'Heh-heh. Are we alone, Professor? It's indescribable,' began the visitor bashfully. '*Parole d'honneur*[12] – nothing like it in twenty-five years,' the character took hold of the button on his trousers, 'would you believe it, Professor, every night, flocks of naked girls. I'm positively enchanted. You're a sorcerer.'

'Hm,' hemmed the preoccupied Philipp Philippovich, peering into the guest's pupils.

The latter finally gained control of his buttons and took off his striped trousers. Beneath them were long johns, the like of which had never been seen. They were cream in colour with black silk cats embroidered on them, and they smelt of perfume.

The dog could not endure the cats and woofed so loud that the character jumped.

'Ooh!'

'I'll give you such a thrashing! Don't be afraid, he doesn't bite.'

'I don't bite?' the dog wondered.

From his trouser pocket the guest dropped onto the carpet a small envelope on which was depicted a beautiful girl with her hair hanging loose. The character jumped, bent down, picked her up and blushed deeply.

'Just you watch out, though,' said Philipp Philippovich cautioningly and sombrely, wagging his finger, 'all the same, watch out, don't overdo it!'

'I'm not over...' the character began mumbling in embarrassment, continuing to get undressed, 'it's only in the way of an experiment, dear Professor.'

'Well, then? What are the results?' asked Philipp Philippovich sternly.

The character waved his hand in ecstasy.

'Nothing like it, I swear to God, Professor, in twenty-five years. The last time was in 1899 in Paris on *rue de la Paix*.'

'And why have you gone green?'

The stranger's face became clouded.

'Damned Zhirkost[13]! You can't imagine, Professor, what those ne'er-do-wells palmed me off with instead of dye. Just look,' mumbled the character, glancing round for a mirror. 'They should have their faces smashed in!' he added, growing furious. 'What ever am I to do now, Professor?' he asked pathetically.

'Ahem, shave your head bare.'

'Professor,' the visitor exclaimed plaintively, 'it'll grow out again grey, won't it? And apart from that, I won't be able to show my face at work, and this is already the third day I've not gone in as it is. The car comes and I let it go. Ah, Professor, if only you could discover a method for rejuvenating hair as well!'

'Not all at once, my dear fellow, not all at once,' mumbled Philipp Philippovich.

Bending down, with shining eyes he examined the patient's bare stomach.

'Well, then – delightful, everything's completely in order. To tell the truth, I hadn't even expected such a result. "A lot of blood, a lot of songs…" Get dressed, my dear fellow!'

' "For the one most charming of all!…" ' the patient joined in, his voice jangling like a frying pan, and, radiant, he began getting dressed. Having put himself in order, jumping up and down and spreading the smell of perfume, he counted out a wad of white notes to Philipp Philippovich and started tenderly squeezing both of his hands.

'You needn't come back for two weeks,' said Philipp Philippovich, 'but I would ask you all the same to be careful.'

'Professor!' a voice exclaimed in ecstasy from beyond the door, 'rest entirely assured,' he tittered sweetly and was lost.

Melodic ringing flew through the apartment, the varnished door opened, in came the bitten one, handed Philipp Philippovich a sheet of paper and declared:

'The age is shown incorrectly. Probably fifty-four or fifty-five. The heart tones are rather indistinct.'

He disappeared and was replaced by a rustling lady in a hat, jauntily cocked to one side, and with a glittering necklace on a withered, chewed-up neck. Strange black bags hung beneath her eyes, but her cheeks were the rosy colour of a doll's. She was highly agitated.

'Madam! How old are you?' Philipp Philippovich asked her very sternly.

The lady took fright and even turned pale underneath the crust of rouge.

'I swear, Professor, if you knew what a drama I'm going through!…'

'How old are you, madam?' Philipp Philippovich repeated even more sternly.

'My word of honour… Well, forty-five…'

'Madam,' Philipp Philippovich wailed, 'people are waiting to see me. Please don't delay things. You're not the only one!'

The lady's breast heaved violently.

'I turn to you alone as a luminary of science. But I swear – it's such a horror…'

'How old are you?' asked Philipp Philippovich, yelping in fury, and his spectacles flashed.

'Fifty-one!' replied the lady, grimacing in fear.

'Take off your pants, madam,' said Philipp Philippovich in relief, and indicated the high, white scaffold in the corner.

'I swear, Professor,' the lady mumbled, undoing with trembling fingers poppers of some kind on her belt, 'this Morits… I confess to you, in all honesty…'

' "From Seville unto Granada…" ' Philipp Philippovich absent-mindedly burst into song and pressed the pedal in the marble washbasin. Water gushed.

'I swear to God!' said the lady, and living blotches of colour forced their way through the artificial ones on her cheeks, 'I know it's my last passion. I mean, he's such a wretch! Oh, Professor! He's a card sharp, the whole of Moscow knows it. He can't let a single vile little milliner go by. He's so devilishly young, you know.' The lady mumbled and threw out from beneath her swishing skirts a crumpled lace rag.

The dog clouded over completely, and everything turned upside down in his head.

'You can go to the devil,' he thought dully, laying his head on his paws and dozing off in shame, 'and I'm not going to try and understand what this is – I won't understand it anyway.'

He came to at the sound of ringing and saw that Philipp Philippovich had flung some shiny tubes of some sort into a basin.

With her hands pressed against her breast, the blotchy lady was gazing hopefully at Philipp Philippovich. The latter knitted his brows weightily and, sitting down at the desk, made a note of something.

'I'm putting a monkey's ovaries in for you, madam,' he announced and gave a severe look.

'Oh, Professor, surely not a monkey's?'

'Yes,' replied Philipp Philippovich unbendingly.

'And when's the operation?' asked the lady in a weak voice, turning pale.

'"From Seville unto Granada…" Ahem… on Monday. You'll be admitted to the clinic first thing in the morning. My assistant will prepare you.'

'Oh, I don't want to go into the clinic. Can't it be done here at home, Professor?'

'I do operations at home, you see, only in extreme cases. It's going to be very expensive – five hundred roubles.'

'Agreed, Professor.'

Again the water roared, a feathered hat fluttered, then a head as bald as a plate appeared and embraced Philipp Philippovich. The dog dozed, the nausea had passed, the dog enjoyed his quietened side and the warmth, and he even had a snore and managed to catch a little bit of a pleasant dream: as if he had ripped an entire tuft of feathers from the owl's tail… then an agitated voice yapped above his head.

'I'm a well-known public figure, Professor. What am I to do now?'

'Gentlemen,' cried Philipp Philippovich indignantly, 'this just isn't the way. Self-control's required. How old is she?'

'Fourteen, Professor... You understand, the publicity will ruin me. In a few days I should be getting an official trip to London.'

'But I'm not a lawyer, you know, my dear fellow... Well, wait for two years and marry her.'

'I'm married, Professor!'

'Oh, gentlemen, gentlemen!'

Doors opened, faces changed, instruments clattered in the cabinet, and Philipp Philippovich worked indefatigably.

'A low life sort of apartment,' thought the dog, 'yet how good it is! But what the devil did he want me for? Will he really keep me living here? What a crankl! I mean, he'd only need to blink and he could set himself up with such a dog, it'd make you gasp! But maybe I'm handsome too. Evidently my good fortune! But that owl's a rotter!... Insolent.'

The dog came round completely deep into the evening when the ringing had stopped, and at precisely the moment when the door admitted some special visitors. There were four of them at once. All young persons, and all dressed very modestly.

'What do this lot want?' thought the dog in surprise. The guests were greeted with much greater hostility by Philipp Philippovich. He stood by the desk and looked at the people who had come in like a military commander at his enemies. The nostrils of his hawkish nose flared. The newcomers marked time on the carpet.

'This, Professor,' began the one on whose head a shock of very thick, wavy hair towered up twenty centimetres, 'is what we've come to see you about...'

'It's a mistake, gentlemen, for you to go about without galoshes in such weather,' Philipp Philippovich interrupted him edifyingly, 'firstly, you'll catch cold, and secondly, you've left dirty marks on my carpets, and all my carpets are Persian.'

The one with the shock fell silent, and all four of them stared at Philipp Philippovich in amazement. The silence lasted several seconds, and it was only broken by the tapping of Philipp Philippovich's fingers on a painted wooden dish on the desk.

'Firstly, we're not gentlemen,' finally said the youngest of the four, who had the appearance of a peach.

'Firstly,' Philipp Philippovich interrupted him too, 'are you a man or a woman?'

The four went silent again and opened their mouths. On this occasion it was the first one, the one with the shock, that came to his senses.

'What difference does it make, comrade?' he asked haughtily.

'I'm a woman,' admitted the peach-like youth in a leather jacket, and blushed. In his turn, and for some reason in the deepest possible way, another of the arrivals blushed – a blond in a Caucasian fur hat.

'In that case you may remain in your cap, but you, my dear sir, I would ask to remove your headgear,' said Philipp Philippovich imposingly.

'I'm not your dear sir,' declared the blond sharply, taking off his fur hat.

'We've come to see you,' the dark one with the shock began once again…

'First of all – who are we?'

'We – the new House Committee of our building,' began the dark one in contained fury. 'I'm Shvonder, she's Vyazemskaya, they're Comrades Pestrukhin and Zharovkin. And so, we…'

'Are you the ones put into Fyodor Pavlovich Sablin's apartment?'

'We are,' replied Shvonder.

'God, it's the end for Kalabukhov's house![14]' exclaimed Philipp Philippovich in despair and clapped his hands together.

'Are you joking, Professor?' said the exasperated Shvonder.

'How can I be joking?! I'm in utter despair,' cried Philipp Philippovich, 'what ever will happen to the central heating now?'

'Are you mocking us, Professor Preobrazhensky?'

'What have you come to see me about? Tell me as quickly as possible, I'm going to have dinner now.'

'We, the House Committee,' began Shvonder with hatred, 'have come to you following a general meeting of the residents of our building, at which the question of the reduction of space in the building's apartments stood...'

'Who stood on whom?' cried Philipp Philippovich, 'be so good as to expound your ideas more clearly.'

'The question of the reduction of space stood.'

'Enough! I understand! Are you aware that by a decree of the 12th of August of this year my apartment is exempt from any reduction of space or resettlement whatsoever?'

'We are,' replied Shvonder, 'but the general meeting, having reviewed your question, came to the conclusion that, in general and as a whole, you occupy an excessive floor area. Utterly excessive. You live alone in seven rooms.'

'I live alone and work in seven rooms,' replied Philipp Philippovich, 'and would like to have an eighth. I need it for use as a library.'

The four of them were dumbstruck.

'An eighth? Eh-heh-heh,' said the blond deprived of his headgear, 'well that's fantastic.'

'It's indescribable!' exclaimed the youth who had turned out to be a woman.

'I have a waiting room – note, it's also the library – dining room, my study – three. A consulting room – four. An operating room – five. My bedroom – six, and the servants' room – seven. All in all, it's not enough... But anyway, that's unimportant. My apartment's exempt, and that's an end to the conversation. Can I go and have dinner?'

'Excuse me,' said the fourth, who resembled a powerful beetle.

'Excuse me,' Shvonder interrupted him, 'it was precisely regarding the dining room and the consulting room that we came to talk. The general meeting requests you voluntarily, by way of labour discipline, to give up the dining room. Nobody in Moscow has dining rooms.'

'Not even Isadora Duncan[15],' cried the woman in a ringing voice.

Something happened to Philipp Philippovich, as a consequence of which his face turned gently crimson, and he did not utter a single sound, waiting for what would come next.

'And the consulting room too,' continued Shvonder, 'the consulting room can be combined perfectly well with the study.'

'Aha,' said Philipp Philippovich in a strange sort of voice, 'and where then should I be taking my food?'

'In the bedroom,' all four of them replied in unison.

Philipp Philippovich's crimsonness took on a somewhat greyish tone.

'Take my food in the bedroom,' he began in a slightly strangulated voice, 'read in the consulting room, get dressed in the waiting room, operate in the servants' room, and conduct examinations in the dining room. It's quite possible that Isadora Duncan does just that. Maybe she has dinner in the study and cuts rabbits open in the bathroom. Maybe. But I'm not Isadora Duncan!...' he suddenly roared, and his crimsonness became yellow. 'I'm going to dine in the dining room and operate in the operating room! Convey that to the general meeting, and I most humbly request you to return to your affairs and allow me the opportunity of taking my food in the place where it is taken by all normal people – that is, in the dining room, and not in the entrance hall, nor in the nursery.'

'Then in view of your stubborn opposition, Professor,' said the agitated Shvonder, 'we shall lodge a complaint against you with higher authorities.'

'Aha,' said Philipp Philippovich, 'really?' And his voice took on a suspiciously polite tone. 'I'll ask you to wait for just one moment.'

'This lad here,' thought the dog in delight, 'is just like me. Ooh, he'll take a bite out of them in a minute, ooh, he'll take a bite. I don't know in what way yet, but he'll take such a bite... Give them one! Grab that lanky one a little way above his boot by the tendon at the back of the knee... r-r-r...'

Philipp Philippovich, after giving it a bang, took the receiver from the telephone and spoke into it thus:

'Please... yes... thank you... May I speak to Vitaly Alexandrovich, please? Professor Preobrazhensky. Vitaly Alexandrovich? Very glad to have caught you. Well, thank you. Vitaly Alexandrovich, your operation is cancelled. What? No, cancelled completely. Just like all other operations. This is why: I'm ceasing my work in Moscow and in Russia as a whole... Four people have just come in to see me, one of them a woman dressed as a man and two of them armed with revolvers, and have been terrorising me in my apartment with the objective of taking a part of it away.'

'Excuse me, Professor,' began Shvonder, changing countenance.

'I'm sorry... I don't have the capacity to repeat all that they said. I'm not a lover of nonsense. Suffice to say that they suggested I give up my consulting room, in other words, forced upon me the necessity of operating on you where up until now I've been cutting rabbits open. In such conditions not only am I unable, I do not even have the right to work. I am therefore ceasing my activity, I am closing my apartment and leaving for Sochi. I can give my keys to Shvonder. Let him operate.'

The four had frozen. The snow was melting on their boots.

'What can one do?... It's very unpleasant for me myself... What? Oh no, Vitaly Alexandrovich! Oh no. I can't consent to it any more. My patience is exhausted. This is already the second occurrence since August. What? Hm... As you please. If only. But just one condition: whoever you please, whenever you please, whatever you please, but it should be a document such that, in the light of it, neither Shvonder nor anyone else could even approach the door of my apartment. A definitive document. Actual. Real! Armour-plating. Such that my name should not even be mentioned. Finished. I'm dead for them. Yes, yes. You're welcome. Who? Aha... Well, that's another matter. Aha... Very well. I'm passing the receiver now. Be so kind,' Philipp Philippovich addressed Shvonder in the voice of a snake, 'you're going to be spoken to now.'

'Excuse me, Professor,' said Shvonder, now flaring up, now dying down, 'you twisted our words.'

'I'll request you not to use such expressions.'

Shvonder took the receiver in bewilderment and said:

'Hello. Yes. Chairman of the House Committee... We were acting in accordance with the rules... But the professor is in a quite exceptional position as it is... We know about his work... We meant to leave him five whole rooms... Well, all right... Since that's how it is... All right...'

Completely red, he hung up the receiver and turned around.

'How he's humiliated him! What a fellow!' thought the dog admiringly. 'What, does he know a special word or something?

Well, you can beat me all you like now, but I won't be leaving here.'

The three looked at the humiliated Shvonder open-mouthed.

'It's a disgrace,' said the latter insecurely.

'If there were a discussion now,' began the woman excitedly, flushing hotly, 'I'd demonstrate to Vitaly Alexandrovich…'

'I'm sorry, but you don't want to open the discussion this very minute?' asked Philipp Philippovich politely.

The woman's eyes flared up.

'I understand your irony, Professor, we'll be going now… Only I, as Director of the House Cultural Section…'

'Di-rec-tress,' Philipp Philippovich corrected her.

'I want to suggest,' here the woman pulled out from her bosom some bright magazines, wet with snow, 'that you take some magazines in aid of the children of France. Fifty kopeks each.'

'No, I won't,' replied Philipp Philippovich curtly, looking askance at the magazines.

Utter astonishment was expressed on the visitors' faces, while the woman was covered with a cranberry patina.

'But why do you refuse?'

'I don't want to.'

'Don't you sympathise with the children of France?'

'I do.'

'Do you begrudge the fifty kopeks each?'

'No.'

'So why then?'

'I don't want to.'

There was a silence.

'You know what, Professor,' began the girl with a heavy sigh, 'if you weren't a European luminary, and you weren't stood up for in the most shocking manner' (the blond tugged at the hem of her jacket, but she brushed him off) 'by figures whom, I'm certain, we shall yet clear up, you ought to be arrested.'

'And what for?' asked Philipp Philippovich curiously.

'You are a hater of the proletariat!' said the woman proudly.

'It's true, I don't like the proletariat,' concurred Philipp Philippovich sadly, and pressed a button. Somewhere there was a ringing. The door into the corridor opened.

'Zina,' called Philipp Philippovich, 'serve dinner. Will you permit me, gentlemen?'

The four of them left the study in silence, went through the waiting room in silence, through the entrance hall in silence, and the front door could be heard closing heavily and sonorously behind them.

The dog rose up onto its hind legs and performed before Philipp Philippovich some sort of ritual of prayer.

3

On plates decorated with heavenly flowers and with a broad black border lay thinly sliced pieces of salmon and pickled eels. On a heavy board was a chunk of cheese with a tear of fat, and in a little silver tub lined with snow – caviar. Between the plates were several delicate little glasses and three small crystal carafes of vodka of various colours. All these objects were fitted onto a small marble table, cosily adjoining a huge sideboard of carved oak, which belched forth pencils of glassy and silvery light. In the middle of the room was a table as heavy as a sepulchre, covered with a white tablecloth, and upon it – two sets of cutlery, napkins folded in the form of papal tiaras and three dark bottles.

Zina brought in a covered silver dish in which something was grumbling. There was such a smell coming from the dish that the dog's mouth immediately filled with runny saliva. 'The gardens of Semiramis[16]!' he thought, and began thumping his tail on the parquet like a stick.

'Bring them here,' commanded Philipp Philippovich predatorily. 'Dr Bormental, leave the caviar alone, I beg you. And if you want to listen to some good advice: rather than the English, pour some ordinary Russian vodka.'

The bitten beauty – he was already out of the white coat, in a decent black suit – jerked his broad shoulders, grinned politely and poured out some colourless vodka.

'The newly blessed[17]?' he enquired.

'Good God, my dear fellow,' the host responded. 'This is spirit. Darya Petrovna makes excellent vodka herself.'

'Oh come now, Philipp Philippovich, everybody maintains it's very decent – thirty degrees.'

'But vodka ought to be forty degrees, and not thirty, that's the first thing,' Philipp Philippovich interrupted admonishingly, 'and secondly – God knows what they've put in it. Can you say what they'll take into their heads?'

'Anything at all,' said the bitten one confidently.

'And I'm of the same opinion,' added Philipp Philippovich, and tossed the contents of the glass into his throat in a single lump, 'm-m-m... Dr Bormental, I beg you, try this little thing instantly, and if you say it's... I'm your deadly enemy for the rest of my life. "From Seville unto Granada..."'

With these words he himself picked up on his palmate silver fork something resembling a small dark piece of bread. The bitten one followed his example. Philipp Philippovich's eyes lit up.

'Is that bad?' asked Philipp Philippovich, chewing. 'Is it? Come on, reply, respected Doctor.'

'It's incomparable,' replied the bitten one sincerely.

'I should say so!... Take note, Ivan Arnoldovich, only land-owners who've not yet had their throats cut by the Bolsheviks have cold hors d'oeuvres and soup. Anyone with the least bit of self-respect operates with hot hors d'oeuvres. And of Moscow's hot hors d'oeuvres – this is number one. There was a time they used to cook them magnificently at the Slavyansky Bazaar[18]. Here, here's yours.'

'You give the dog food in the dining room,' a female voice was heard, 'and then nothing will get him out of here.'

'It's all right. The poor thing's starving.' On the end of his fork Philipp Philippovich offered the dog some hors d'oeuvre, which was taken by the latter with the deftness of a conjuror, then he threw the fork down with a clatter into the slop-basin.

Thereafter from the plates there rose steam smelling of crawfish; the dog sat in the shadow of the tablecloth with the look of a sentry by a powder store. And Philipp Philippovich, having tucked the tight tail of a napkin into his collar, was preaching:

'Food, Ivan Arnoldovich, is an intricate thing. You need to know how to eat, but imagine – the majority of people don't know how to eat at all. Not only do you need to know what to eat, but also when and how.' (Philipp Philippovich shook his spoon meaningfully.) 'And what to say when doing so. Yes, sir. If you're concerned about your digestion, my good advice is not to talk over dinner about Bolshevism or about medicine. And – God preserve you – don't read the Soviet newspapers before dinner.'

'Hm... But then there aren't any others.'

'So don't you read any then. You know, I've carried out thirty observations in my clinic. And what do you think? The patients who don't read the newspapers feel splendid. But those I intentionally forced to read *Pravda* lost weight.'

'Hm...' the bitten one responded with interest, turning pink from the soup and the wine.

'And that's not all. Diminished knee reflexes, poor appetite, depression.'

'The devil...'

'Yes, sir. But whatever am I doing? I've started talking about medicine myself. Better let's just eat.'

Leaning back, Philipp Philippovich rang the bell, and Zina appeared in the cherry-red door-curtain. The dog got a pale, thick piece of sturgeon which he did not like, and directly after it a slice of bloody roast beef. After gobbling it up, the dog suddenly felt he wanted to sleep and could not look at any more food. 'A strange sensation,' he thought, shutting his newly heavy eyelids, 'my eyes couldn't bear to look at food of any sort. But smoking after dinner – that's stupid.'

The dining room filled up with unpleasant blue smoke. The dog dozed with his head settled on his front paws.

'St Julien's a decent wine,' heard the dog in his sleep, 'only there isn't any of it now, you know.'

A muffled chorale, softened by ceilings and carpets, carried from somewhere above and to the side.

Philipp Philippovich rang the bell and Zina came.

'Zinusha, what does that mean?'

'They've made a general meeting again, Philipp Philippovich,' replied Zina.

'Again!' exclaimed Philipp Philippovich mournfully, 'well, so now it's under way, and Kalabukhov's house is done for. I'll have to move out, but where to, one asks? Everything will go swimmingly. To begin with, there'll be singing every evening, next the pipes will freeze up in the loos, then the central heating boiler will burst, and so on. It's the end for Kalabukhov.'

'Philipp Philippovich is grieving,' remarked Zina, smiling, and took away a pile of plates.

'How can one help but grieve?!' cried Philipp Philippovich. 'I mean, what a house it used to be – you must understand!'

'You look at things too gloomily, Philipp Philippovich,' retorted the bitten beauty, 'they've altered radically now.'

'My dear fellow, you do know me? Don't you? I'm a man of facts, a man of observation. I'm an enemy of unfounded hypotheses. And that's very well known not only in Russia, but in Europe too. If I say something, that means the basis is a certain fact from which I draw a conclusion. And here's a fact for you: the coat stand and galosh rack in our house.'

'That's interesting...'

'Galoshes are rubbish. Happiness doesn't come from galoshes,' thought the dog, 'but he's an outstanding personality.'

'If you please – the galosh stand. I've been living in this building since 1903. And so, over the course of that period, until April 1917, there was not one instance – I underline it in red pencil, *not one* – of even one pair of galoshes disappearing out of our main entrance downstairs with its shared, unlocked door. Take note, there are twelve apartments here, I have surgery hours. One fine day in April 1917 all the galoshes disappeared, including two pairs of mine, three sticks, an overcoat and the doorman's samovar. And since that time the galosh stand has ceased to exist. My dear fellow! I'm no longer talking about the central heating. I'm not. So be it: social revolution, so no need for heating. Although some day, if I have the time, I'll do some research on the brain and demonstrate that all this social upheaval is quite simply the ravings of the sick... So what I'm saying is: why, when this whole business began, did everyone start walking up and down the marble staircase in dirty galoshes and felt boots? Why is it still necessary to this day to lock galoshes up? And in addition to set a soldier over them so that nobody can swipe them? Why was the carpet taken away from the main staircase? Does Karl Marx[19] forbid the keeping of carpets on the stairs? Does it say somewhere in Karl Marx that entrance number two in the Kalabukhov House on Prechistenka should be boarded up and you should go round through the backyard? Who needs that? Oppressed negroes? Or the workers of Portugal? Why can't a proletarian leave his galoshes downstairs, instead of dirtying the marble?'

'But Philipp Philippovich, I mean, he doesn't have any galoshes at all,' the bitten one tried to get a word in.

'Nothing of the sort!' replied Philipp Philippovich in a thunderous voice, and poured a glass of wine. 'Hm... I don't approve of liqueurs after dinner: they make you put on weight and have a bad effect upon the liver... Nothing of the kind! He does have galoshes on now, and those galoshes... are mine! Precisely those very galoshes that disappeared on the 13th of April 1917.[20] Who nicked them, one wonders? Did I? Impossible. Sablin the bourgeois?' (Philipp Philippovich poked his finger towards the ceiling.) 'It's ridiculous even to suppose it. Polozov, the sugar refinery man?' (Philipp Philippovich indicated to one side.) 'Under no circumstances! It was done by those very songsters! Yes, sir! But they could at least take them off on the staircase!' (Philipp Philippovich began to go crimson.) 'What the devil did they take the flowers away from the landings for? Why does the electricity – which, if my memory serves me well, went off twice in the course of twenty years – these days go off punctually once a month? Dr Bormental, statistics are a dreadful thing. You, who are familiar with my latest work, are better aware of that than anyone.'

'It's the collapse, Philipp Philippovich...'

'No,' objected Philipp Philippovich with complete certainty, 'no. You be the first, dear Ivan Arnoldovich, to refrain from using that particular word. It's a mirage, smoke, a fiction,' Philipp Philippovich spread his short fingers wide, as a result of which two shadows resembling tortoises began crawling over the tablecloth. 'What is this collapse of yours? An old woman with a stick? A witch who has knocked out all the window panes and put out all the lamps? It just doesn't exist at all. What are you implying with that word?' Philipp Philippovich enquired furiously of an unfortunate cardboard duck hanging upside down next to the sideboard, and answered on its behalf himself: 'This is what: if I, instead of operating every evening, begin singing in a choir in my apartment, I'll start to suffer a collapse. If I, going into the lavatory, begin – forgive the expression – urinating outside the toilet bowl, and Zina and Darya Petrovna do the same, a collapse will start in the lavatory. Therefore the collapse is not in WCs, but in heads. So when these baritones shout: "Beat the collapse!" – I laugh.' (Philipp Philippovich's face had become so contorted that the bitten one was open-mouthed.) 'I swear to you, I find it funny! That means every one of them ought to be bashing himself on the back of the head! And then, when he's bashed world revolution, Engels and Nikolai Romanov,[21] oppressed Malaysians and other such hallucinations out of himself and made a start on cleaning the sheds – his real work – the collapse will disappear by itself. You can't serve two gods! It's impossible at one and the same time to sweep the tramlines and organise the fates of some Spanish ragamuffins! No one will succeed in that, Doctor, and especially not people who are in general lagging some two hundred years behind the Europeans in their development and are to this day still not entirely confident about doing up their own trousers!'

Philipp Philippovich had grown excited. His hawkish nostrils flared. Having grown in strength after a substantial dinner, he thundered like an ancient prophet and his head flashed silver.

His words fell upon the sleepy dog like a muffled, underground rumbling. Now the owl with silly yellow eyes would leap out in his sleepy vision, now the vile, ugly mug of the butcher in the dirty white cap, now Philipp Philippovich's dashing moustache, lit by the sharp electricity from the lampshade, now sleepy sledges creaked and disappeared, while in the dog's stomach the mangled piece of roast beef, floating in juice, was being digested.

'He could earn money right there at rallies,' dreamt the dog dimly, 'a top-class operator. But he's clearly rolling in money as it is.'

'A policeman!' shouted Philipp Philippovich. 'A policeman!!' – 'Ow-bow-wow!' bubbles of some kind were bursting in the dog's brain... 'A policeman! That and that alone. And it's utterly irrelevant whether he's wearing a metal badge or a red kepi. Stand a policeman next to everyone and make the policeman moderate the vocal outbursts of our citizens. You say – the collapse. I tell you, Doctor, that nothing will change for the better in our house, nor in any other house, until our singers have been quietened down! As soon as they cease their concerts, the situation will change for the better by itself.'

'They're counter-revolutionary things you're saying, Philipp Philippovich,' remarked the bitten one jokingly. 'God forbid anyone should hear you.'

'Nothing dangerous,' retorted Philipp Philippovich hotly. 'No counter-revolution. Incidentally, there's another word I simply can't bear. It's a complete mystery what's hidden behind it. The devil knows! So what I'm saying is: there's none of this counter-revolution in my words. There's common sense in them and life experience.'

At this point Philipp Philippovich took out from his collar the tail of the shining, crumpled napkin and, screwing it up, he put it down next to his unfinished glass of wine. The bitten one immediately rose and said thank you: '*Merci.*'

'One moment, Doctor!' Philipp Philippovich checked him, taking his wallet out of his trouser pocket. He narrowed his eyes, counted out some white notes and reached them out to the bitten one with the words: 'Today, Ivan Arnoldovich, you're due forty roubles. Here.'

The dog's victim thanked him politely and, blushing, pushed the money into his jacket pocket.

'Don't you need me this evening, Philipp Philippovich?' he enquired.

'Thank you, my dear fellow, no. We shan't do anything today. Firstly, the rabbit's dead, and secondly, it's *Aïda* today at the Bolshoi. And I've not heard it for a long time. I love it… Do you remember? The duet… Tari-ra-rim.'

'How do you find the time, Philipp Philippovich?' asked the doctor respectfully.

'The man who hurries nowhere has time for everything,' explained his host edifyingly. 'Of course, if I began hopping from one meeting to another and singing songs all day like a nightingale, instead of getting on with my real work, I wouldn't have time for anything,' beneath Philipp Philippovich's fingers his repeater began its heavenly chiming in his pocket, 'Just gone eight o'clock… I'll go for the start of the second act… I'm a supporter of the division of labour. Let them sing at the Bolshoi, and I'll do operations. That's the way. And no collapses… I'll tell you what, Ivan Arnoldovich, you keep a careful lookout all the same: as soon as there's a suitable death, off of the table at once – into the nutritional liquid and to me!'

'Don't worry, Philipp Philippovich, the pathologico-anatomists have promised me.'

'Excellent, and in the meantime we'll carry out some observation of this neurasthenic of the streets. Let his side heal.'

'He's concerned for me,' thought the dog, 'he's a very good man. I know who he is. He's a magician, the wizard and sorcerer from a dog's fairytale… I mean, it simply can't be that I've dreamt all this. But what if it is a dream?' (The dog shuddered in his sleep.) 'I'll wake up… and there's nothing. No lamp in silk, no warmth, no full stomach. It'll all start again, the gateway, the terrible cold, the frozen asphalt, the hunger, the wicked people… The canteen, the snow… God, how hard I'll find it!…'

4

But none of this happened. The gateway in particular melted away like a loathsome dream and returned no more.

Evidently the collapse was not so very terrible. Irrespective of it, twice a day the grey concertinas under the window sill were flooded with heat, and warmth spread in waves throughout the entire apartment.

Quite clearly, the dog had drawn the winning canine ticket. No less than twice a day now his eyes filled with tears of gratitude directed towards the sage of Prechistenka. Besides that, all the cheval-glasses in the drawing room, in the waiting room between the cabinets, reflected a lucky, handsome dog.

'I'm a handsome one. Perhaps an unknown dog-prince incognito,' mused the dog, gazing at the shaggy, coffee-coloured dog with the contented face, strolling in the mirrored distances. 'It's very likely that my grandmother transgressed with a Newfoundland. Look at that, there's a white patch on my face. Where's it from, one wonders? Philipp Philippovich is a man of great taste, he won't take the first mongrel he comes across.'

In the course of a week the dog ate up as much as he had in the last hungry month and a half on the street. Well, only in weight, of course. Of the quality of food at Philipp Philippovich's there was nothing to be said. Even without taking into consideration the fact that a heap of scraps was bought in daily by Darya Petrovna at the Smolensk Market for eighteen kopeks, it is sufficient to mention the dinners at seven o'clock in the evening in the dining room at which the dog was present, in spite of the protests of the elegant Zina. During these dinners Philipp Philippovich was conclusively awarded the rank of a divinity. The dog stood up on his hind legs and chewed his jacket, the dog learnt Philipp Philippovich's way of ringing – two of the master's sonorous, abrupt blows, and he flew out barking to meet him in the entrance hall. The master would burst in wearing his black-brown fox, sparkling with a million snowy spangles, smelling of mandarins, cigars, perfume, lemons, petrol, eau de cologne, cloth – and his voice, like a megaphone, carried all through the dwelling.

'Why have you ripped the owl apart, you swine? Was it bothering you? Was it, I'm asking you? Why have you broken Professor Mechnikov[22]?'

'He should be flogged with a whip, Philipp Philippovich, once at least,' said Zina indignantly, 'or else he'll be completely ruined. Just you look what he's done with your galoshes.'

'No one should be flogged,' fretted Philipp Philippovich, 're-member that once and for all. One can have an effect on men and on animals only by suggestion. Has he been given some meat today?'

'Good Lord, he's guzzled down all there was in the house. Why do you have to ask, Philipp Philippovich? I'm amazed he doesn't burst.'

'Well, let him eat as he pleases... What had the owl done to you, you hooligan?'

'Ow-ow!' whined the toadying dog, and crawled on his belly with his paws turned outwards.

An uproar followed, as he was dragged by the scruff of the neck through the waiting room into the study. The dog whimpered, snapped, caught hold of the carpet, rode on his bottom like in the circus. In the middle of the study on the carpet lay the glass-eyed owl with a ripped stomach, out of which protruded some red rags smelling of mothballs. On the desk lay a portrait, smashed to smithereens.

'I didn't clear up on purpose, so you could admire it,' reported Zina, upset. 'He leapt up onto the desk, you know, the wretch! And grabbed it by the tail! I hadn't had time to recover myself before he'd torn the whole thing to pieces. Poke his face into the owl, Philipp Philippovich, so he knows what it is to ruin things.'

And the howling began. The dog, who was stuck to the carpet, was pulled up to be poked into the owl, at which the dog was in floods of bitter tears, thinking: 'Beat me, only don't throw me out of the apartment.'

'Send the owl to the taxidermist today. In addition, here you are, eight roubles plus sixteen kopeks for the tram, go to Muir's[23] and buy him a good collar with a chain.'

The following day they put a wide, shiny collar on the dog. The first moment after looking at himself in the mirror he was very upset, and went off into the bathroom with his tail between his legs, pondering how he could rip it off against a trunk or a chest. But he very quickly realised he was simply a fool. Zina took him for a walk on the chain. The dog walked down Obukhov Lane like a prisoner, burning up with shame, but after going along Prechistenka as far as the Church of Christ, he got an excellent grasp of what a collar means in life. Rabid envy could be read in the eyes of all the dogs they met, and by Myortvy Lane some lanky mongrel with a docked tail barked out that he was a 'posh bastard' and an 'arse-licker'. As they were cutting across the tram rails, a policeman looked at the collar with pleasure and respect, and when they returned, the most unseen thing in life occurred: Fyodor the doorman personally opened the front door and let Sharik in. At the same time he remarked to Zina:

'Just look at what a shaggy one Philipp Philippovich has found himself. And he's amazingly fat.'

'I should think so – he scoffs enough for six,' explained Zina, rosy and pretty from the frost.

'A collar's just as good as a briefcase,' quipped the dog in his head and, waggling his backside, set off for the *bel' étage* as if he owned the place.

Having appreciated the true value of a collar, the dog made his first visit to the most important section of heaven, entry into which had until now been categorically forbidden him – namely, into the realm of the cook, Darya Petrovna. The entire apartment was not worth even a couple of feet of Darya's realm. Every day in the tiled stove with a black top the flame spat and raged. The oven crackled. In crimson columns Darya Petrovna's face burnt with eternal fiery torment and unquenched passion. It was shiny and shot with fat. In the fashionable hairstyle that covered her ears and had a basket of fair hair at the back of her head gleamed twenty-two imitation diamonds. On hooks around the walls hung gold saucepans, the entire kitchen rumbled with smells, gurgled and hissed in closed vessels...

'Out!' wailed Darya Petrovna. 'Out, you stray pickpocket! You're all that's needed here! I'll give you one with the poker!...'

'What's wrong with you? Well, what are you snarling about?' the dog narrowed his eyes ingratiatingly. 'What sort of pickpocket am I? Haven't you noticed the collar then?' and, poking his face through, he tried to get into the door sideways.

Sharik the dog possessed some sort of secret for winning people's hearts. Two days later he already lay next to the basket of coal, watching Darya Petrovna working. With a sharp, slender knife she chopped the heads and feet off helpless hazel grouse, then, like a frenzied executioner, she pulled the flesh off the bones, ripped out the innards from chickens, turned stuff round and round in the mincing machine. Sharik at this time was tearing a grouse's head to pieces. From a bowl of milk Darya Petrovna pulled pieces of soaked white bread, she mixed them on a board with the meat pulp, poured cream over it all, sprinkled with salt and formed rissoles on the board. There was a humming in the stove like at a conflagration, and on the frying pan there was a grumbling, a bubbling and a jumping.

The stove door jumped aside with a crash and revealed a terrible hell in which the flame gurgled and flickered.

In the evening the stone mouth died down, in the kitchen window above the white half-curtain stood the dense and weighty Prechistenka night with its solitary star. In the kitchen it was damp on the floor, the saucepans shone mysteriously and dimly, on the table lay a fireman's cap. Sharik lay on the warm stove like a lion on a gatepost, and, with one ear cocked in curiosity, watched a black-whiskered and excited man in a wide leather belt embracing Darya Petrovna behind the half-closed door in Zina and Darya Petrovna's room. The latter's face burnt with torment and passion, all of it except for the deathly, powdered nose. A strip of light lay on a portrait of the black-whiskered man, and an Easter wreath dangled from it.

'Keeps on at me like a demon,' mumbled Darya Petrovna in the semi-darkness, 'leave me alone! Zina'll be here in a minute. What's going on, it's just like you've been rejuvenated too.'

'We don't need any of that,' replied the black-whiskered man hoarsely and not entirely in control of himself. 'How fiery you are!'

In the evenings the Prechistenka star hid behind the heavy curtains and, if there was no *Aïda* at the Bolshoi Theatre and no meeting of the All-Russian Society of Surgeons, the divinity was to be found in a deep armchair in the study. There were no lights at ceiling level. Just one green lamp burnt on the table. Sharik lay on the carpet in shadow and, unable to tear himself away, gazed upon awful things. In repulsive, pungent and turbid swill in glass vessels lay human brains. The divinity's arms, bared to the elbow, were in ginger-coloured rubber gloves, and slippery, blunt fingers fiddled about in convolutions. At times the divinity armed himself with a small, glittering knife and quietly cut up the yellow, spongy brains.

' "To the sacred banks of the Nile[24]," ' sang the divinity quietly, biting his lips and recalling the golden interior of the Bolshoi Theatre.

The pipes at this hour warmed up to the highest degree. The warmth from them rose to the ceiling, from there it spread throughout the entire room, and in the dog's coat the last flea came to life, yet to be combed out by Philipp Philippovich himself, but already doomed. Carpets muffled the sounds in the apartment. And then far away the front door rang.

'Zinka's gone to the cinematograph,' thought the dog, 'but when she comes back, I expect we'll have supper. It's veal cutlets today, I reckon!'

* * *

And so on that awful day Sharik had already felt a prick of foreboding first thing in the morning. As a consequence of this he had suddenly begun to feel miserable and had eaten his breakfast – half a cup of oat porridge and the previous day's mutton bone – without any appetite at all. He had taken a miserable walk into the waiting room and had a whimper there at his own reflection. But in the afternoon, after Zina had taken him for a walk to the boulevard, the day began to go as usual. There were no surgery hours that day, because, as one knows, there are never surgery hours on Tuesdays, and the divinity was sitting in the study with some heavy books of some sort containing brightly coloured pictures lying open on the desk. They were waiting for dinner. The dog was somewhat enlivened by the thought that the main course today, as he had found out for sure in the kitchen, would be turkey. Walking down the corridor, the dog heard the telephone ring unpleasantly and unexpectedly in Philipp Philippovich's study. Philipp Philippovich picked up the receiver, listened closely and suddenly became excited.

'Excellent,' his voice could be heard, 'bring it right away now, right away!'

He began bustling about, rang the bell, and, when she came in, ordered Zina to serve dinner urgently.

'Dinner! Dinner! Dinner!'

In the dining room plates immediately began to be clattered, Zina began running about, from the kitchen Darya Petrovna could be heard grumbling that the turkey was not ready. Again the dog felt agitated.

'I don't like any commotion in the apartment,' he pondered... And no sooner had he thought this, than the commotion took on a still more unpleasant character. And above all, thanks to the appearance of the once bitten Dr Bormental. He had brought with him a nasty-smelling suitcase and, without even taking his coat off, he sped with it across the corridor into the consulting room. Philipp Philippovich abandoned his unfinished cup of coffee, something that he never did, and ran out to meet Bormental, something that he never did either.

'When did he die?' he cried.

'Three hours ago,' replied Bormental as he undid the suitcase, without taking off his snow-covered hat.

'Who is it that's died?' thought the dog, sullenly and discontentedly, and got under their feet, 'I can't stand it when they rush about.'

'Get out from under my feet! Quick, quick, quick!' cried Philipp Philippovich in all directions and began ringing all the bells, as it seemed to the dog.

Zina came running.

'Zina! Darya Petrovna to the telephone, she's to take messages, no one to be received! You I need. Dr Bormental, I beg you – quick, quick, quick!

'I don't like it, I don't,' frowned the dog, aggrieved, and

began wandering around the apartment, while all the bustle was concentrated in the consulting room. Zina appeared unexpectedly in a white coat resembling a shroud and started running from the consulting room to the kitchen and back.

'Shall I go and eat, then? To hell with them,' decided the dog, and suddenly got a surprise.

'Don't give Sharik anything,' thundered the command from the consulting room.

'And how will you keep an eye on him?'

'Lock him up!'

And Sharik was lured and locked into the bathroom.

'What a cheek,' thought Sharik, sitting in the semi-darkness of the bathroom, 'this is just stupid...'

And he spent about a quarter of an hour in the bathroom in a strange temper – now angry, now in a deep sort of depression. Everything was miserable, obscure...

'You wait, you're going to get galoshes tomorrow, highly respected Philipp Philippovich,' he thought, 'you've had to buy two new pairs already, and now you'll be buying another. So you don't go locking dogs up.'

But all of a sudden his furious thought was interrupted. For some reason, suddenly and clearly, a fragment of his very earliest youth came to mind – the sunny, boundless courtyard by the Preobrazhenskaya Gate, slivers of sunlight in bottles, broken bricks, free and easy vagrant dogs.

'No, where would you go, you won't leave here for any sort of freedom, why lie about it,' grieved the dog, breathing heavily through the nose, 'I've got used to it. I'm a master's dog, an intellectual being, I've tasted a better life. And what's freedom anyway? It's nothing, smoke, a mirage, a fiction... The ravings of those ill-starred democrats...'

Then the semi-darkness of the bathroom became frightening, he began howling, threw himself at the door, started scratching.

'Ow-ow-ow!' flew through the apartment as into a barrel.

'I'll tear the owl to bits again,' thought the dog in an impotent frenzy. Then he weakened and lay still for a while, but when he got up, his coat suddenly stood on end: in the bath for some reason he imagined he could see the repulsive eyes of a wolf.

And at the very height of his torment the door opened up. The dog gave himself a shake, walked out and morosely headed for the kitchen, but Zina drew him insistently by the collar into the consulting room. A chill passed through the dog's heart.

'What do they need me for?' he thought suspiciously. 'My side's healed, I don't understand it at all.'

And he rode on his paws over the slippery parquet, and that was how he was brought into the consulting room. The unprecedented lighting inside it was immediately striking. The white globe just below the ceiling was so radiant, it hurt the eyes. In white radiance stood a high priest and through his teeth he sang about the sacred banks of the Nile. Only by the indistinct scent could this be recognised as Philipp Philippovich. His cropped grey hair was hidden beneath a white cap, reminiscent of a patriarch's cowl; the divinity was all in white, but on top of the white, like an ecclesiastical stole, a narrow rubber apron had been put on. His hands were in black gloves.

The bitten one proved to be wearing a cowl too. The long table had been opened out, and a small, rectangular one on a shiny leg had been moved up close to it on one side.

Most of all the dog felt hatred here for the bitten one, and most of all because of his eyes that day. Usually bold and direct, now they darted away from the dog's eyes in every direction. They were on their guard, false, and in their depths lurked a bad, nasty business, if not an entire crime. The dog glanced at him severely and sullenly and went away into a corner.

'The collar, Zina,' said Philipp Philippovich quietly, 'only don't upset him.'

Zina instantly had eyes just as loathsome as the bitten one's. She went up to the dog and stroked him in an obviously false way.

'Well then... there are three of you. You'll take me if you want. Only you should be ashamed... If only I knew what you were going to do with me...'

Zina undid the collar, the dog gave his head a shake, snorted. The bitten one rose up before him, and a nasty, confusing scent emanated from him.

'Ugh, disgusting... Why do I feel so confused and afraid...' thought the dog, and moved back away from the bitten one.

'Quickly, Doctor,' said Philipp Philippovich impatiently.

There was a sharp and sweet smell in the air. The bitten one, without taking his guarded and horrible eyes from the dog, thrust his right hand out from behind his back and quickly poked a ball of damp cotton wool into the dog's nose. Sharik was dumbfounded, there was a gentle spinning in his head, but he still managed to recoil. The bitten one jumped after him and suddenly plastered cotton wool all over his face. His breathing was immediately blocked, but again the dog managed to break away. 'Villain...' flashed through his head. 'Why?' And once again it was plastered on. At this point, in the middle of the consulting room, a lake unexpectedly presented itself, and upon it, in boats, some very cheerful, fantastic pink dogs from beyond the grave. His legs lost their bones and buckled.

'Onto the table!' Philipp Philippovich's words boomed somewhere in a cheerful voice and ran in orange streams. Horror disappeared, was replaced by joy. For a couple of seconds the failing dog loved the bitten one. Next the whole world turned upside down, and a cold, but pleasant hand was felt under his stomach too. And then – nothing.

Stretched out on the narrow operating table lay Sharik the dog, and his head beat impotently against the white oilskin pillow. His stomach had been sheared, and now Dr Bormental, breathing heavily and hurrying, eating into the coat with his clippers, was shaving the hair on Sharik's head. With his palms resting on the edge of the table, Philipp Philippovich – his eyes shining like the gold rims of his spectacles – was observing this process and saying excitedly:

'Ivan Arnoldovich, the most important moment is when I go into the Turkish saddle. Instantly, I beg you, let me have the appendage and start stitching straight away. If haemorrhaging starts at that point, we'll lose time and we'll lose the dog. But then he has no chance anyway,' he was silent for a moment, narrowed his eye, glanced into the eye of the dog, half-open as if in mockery, and added: 'Do you know, I feel sorry for him. Can you imagine, I've grown used to him.'

He was raising his hands at this point, as though giving Sharik the ill-starred dog his blessing for a difficult feat. He was trying to keep even a single speck of dust from falling onto the black rubber.

From beneath the sheared coat the off-white skin of the dog began to gleam. Bormental tossed aside the clippers and armed himself with a razor. He soaped the impotent little head and started shaving. There was a mighty crunching beneath the blade, in places blood appeared. Having shaved the head, the bitten one wiped it over with a little petrol-soaked ball, then stretched the dog's bared stomach out and pronounced, panting: 'Ready.'

Zina turned on the tap above the sink and Bormental rushed to wash his hands. Zina poured spirit over them from a phial.

'May I leave, Philipp Philippovich?' she asked, looking sidelong and fearfully at the dog's shaved head.

'You may.'

Zina disappeared, Bormental carried on bustling about. He surrounded Sharik's head with light gauze tissues, and then on the pillow there appeared a bald dog's skull, not seen by anyone before, and a strange bearded face.

At this point the high priest stirred. He straightened up, glanced at the dog's head and said:

'Well, Lord, bless us. Knife.'

From the gleaming pile on the little table Bormental pulled a small, fat-bladed knife and handed it to the high priest. Then he clothed himself in just such black gloves as the high priest wore.

'Asleep?' asked Philipp Philippovich.

'Fast asleep.'

Philipp Philippovich's teeth gritted, his small eyes acquired a sharp, prickly lustre, and, with a flourish of the knife, he extended a long and well-aimed incision down Sharik's stomach. The skin parted straight away, and blood splashed out of it in various directions. Bormental threw himself at it predatorily, began pressing on Sharik's incision with balls of gauze, then, with little forceps like sugar tongs, he squeezed its edges together and it dried up. On Bormental's forehead sweat broke out in little bubbles. Philipp Philippovich slashed a second time, and the two of them began to tear Sharik's body apart with hooks, scissors, clamps of some sort. Pink and yellow tissues popped out, weeping with bloody dew. Philipp Philippovich twisted the knife inside the body, then cried: 'Scissors!'

The instrument flashed through the hands of the bitten one as though he were a conjuror. Philipp Philippovich plunged into the depths and in a few turns tore out of Sharik's body his seminal glands together with some scraps of some sort.

Bormental, wet through from zeal and agitation, rushed to a glass jar and drew from it some other, wet, drooping seminal glands. In the hands of the professor and his assistant short, moist strings began to leap and coil. Curved needles set up a staccato clicking inside the clips, the seminal glands were sewn into the place where Sharik's had been. The high priest fell back from the incision, poked a ball of gauze into it and commanded:

'Stitch the skin up instantly, Doctor,' then glanced back at the round white wall clock.

'It took us fourteen minutes,' Bormental let out through clenched teeth, and stuck his curved needle into the flaccid skin. Then both became agitated like murderers in a hurry.

'Knife!' cried Philipp Philippovich.

A knife leapt into his hands as if by itself, after which Philipp Philippovich's face became terrible. He bared his porcelain and gold crowns, and with a single movement drew a red wreath on Sharik's forehead. The skin with the shaved hair was thrown aside like a scalp. The skull was bared. Philipp Philippovich cried:

'Trepan!'

Bormental handed him a shining drill. Biting his lips, Philipp Philippovich began sticking the drill in and boring little holes in Sharik's skull at a distance of a centimetre one from another such that they went around the entire skull. On each he spent no more than five seconds. Then, with a saw of unprecedented form, having shoved its tail into the first little hole, he began sawing in the way a lady's needlework box is sawn up. The skull quietly squealed and shook. After about three minutes the top of Sharik's skull was removed.

Then the dome of Sharik's brain was bared – grey with bluish veins and reddish patches. Philipp Philippovich ate into the membranes with his scissors and opened them up.

Once a fine fountain of blood sprang out, almost hitting the professor in the eye and bespattering his cap. Bormental leapt like a tiger with artery forceps to clamp it, and did. Sweat poured from Bormental in torrents and his face became fleshy and blotched. His eyes darted from the professor's hands to a dish on the instrument table. Meanwhile Philipp Philippovich became positively terrifying. Wheezing sounds ripped from his nose, his teeth were bared to the gums. He stripped the membrane from the brain and set off somewhere into the depths, pulling the hemispheres of the brain out from the opened pan. At that moment Bormental began to turn pale, gripped Sharik's chest with one hand and said rather croakily:

'The pulse is falling sharply...'

Philipp Philippovich glanced round at him bestially, mumbled something and cut in still deeper. With a crunch Bormental broke open a small glass ampoule, sucked a full syringe up from it and perfidiously injected Sharik somewhere near the heart.

'I'm getting towards the Turkish saddle,' growled Philipp Philippovich, and with bloodied, slippery gloves he pulled Sharik's greyish-yellow brain out of his head. For an instant he narrowed his eyes at Sharik's face, and Bormental immediately broke open a second ampoule of yellow liquid and drew it into a long syringe.

'Into the heart?' he asked timidly.

'Why do you have to ask?!' roared the professor viciously. 'You've already had him dead five times anyway. Inject! Is it thinkable?' At this his face became like that of an inspired brigand.

With all his might the doctor easily sank the needle into the heart of the dog.

'He's alive, but only just,' he whispered timidly.

'There's no time for debate here – is he alive or isn't he,' wheezed the terrible Philipp Philippovich. 'I'm at the saddle. He'll die anyway... oh, damna... "To the sacred banks of the Nile..." Let me have the appendage.'

Bormental handed him a bottle in which a small white ball bobbed on a thread in some liquid. – 'He has no equal in Europe, honest to God!' thought Bormental vaguely. With one hand Philipp Philippovich pulled out the bobbing ball, while with the other he cut out a similar one with scissors somewhere in the depths between the pinned-out hemispheres. Sharik's ball he flung out onto a dish, while he put the new one into the brain together with the thread, and with his short fingers, which as if by a miracle had become slender and flexible, he contrived to wind it in there with an amber thread. After that he threw some clamps and forceps out of Sharik's head, put the brain back away again into its bony pan, leant back and asked, already a little more calmly:

'He's dead, of course?...'

'Sketchy pulse,' replied Bormental.

'More adrenalin.'

The professor threw the membranes over the brain, affixed the sawn-off roof as if it were made to measure, pulled the scalp over and let out a roar:

'Stitch it up!'

In about five minutes, having broken three needles, Bormental had stitched the head up.

And so there appeared on the pillow, against a background stained with blood, the lifeless, extinguished face of Sharik with a circular wound on the head. And at this point Philipp Philippovich pulled away fully, like a sated vampire, he tore off one glove, throwing out from it a cloud of sweaty powder, tore the other apart, flung it on the floor and pressed the button in the wall to ring. Zina appeared on the threshold with her back turned so as not to see Sharik covered in blood. With chalked hands the high priest removed his bloodied cowl and cried:

'Get me a cigarette straight away, Zina. A set of fresh linen and a bath.'

He lay his chin on the edge of the table, opened the dog's right eyelid with two fingers, glanced into the clearly dying eye and said:

'So, damn it. Not dead. Well, he'll die all the same. Ah, Dr Bormental, I feel sorry for the dog, he was affectionate, albeit a sly one.'

5

Dr Ivan Arnoldovich Bormental's notebook. Slim, writing-paper size. Filled in Bormental's handwriting. On the first two pages it is neat, small and legible, subsequently bold, excited, with a large number of blots.

Monday, 22nd December 1924

Case history

Laboratory dog approximately 2 years of age, male. Breed – mongrel. Name – Sharik. Coat sparse, matted, brownish, dappled. Tail the colour of baked milk. On the right side traces of fully healed scalding. Nourishment before joining the professor – poor; after a week's stay – extremely well fed. Weight 8 kg. (*exclamation mark*).

Heart, lungs, stomach, temperature normal...

23 December. At 8.30 in the evening Europe's first operation using method of Prof Preobrazhensky performed: under chloroform anaesthetic Sharik's testicles removed, and transplanted in their place human male testicles with appendages and spermatic ducts, taken from a man of 28 years, deceased 4 hours and 4 minutes before operation, and preserved in sterilised physiological liquid using method of Prof Preobrazhensky.

Immediately thereafter, following trepanation of top of skull, cerebral appendage, pituitary gland, removed and replaced with human one from aforementioned man.

Introduced were 8 cc of chloroform, 1 syringe of camphor, plus 2 syringes of adrenalin into heart.

Explanation of operation: performance of Preobrazhensky's experiment with combined pituitary gland and testicle transplant for elucidation of question of body's acceptance of pituitary gland, and subsequently also of its influence on rejuvenation of the organism in humans.

Operating – Prof P.P. Preobrazhensky.

Assisting – Dr I.A. Bormental.

During night after operation: repeated dangerous deterioration of pulse. Expectation of fatal outcome. Huge doses of camphor using method of Preobrazhensky.

24 *December*. In morning – improvement. Respiratory rate doubled, temperature 42. Camphor, caffeine subcutaneously.

25 *December*. Again deterioration. Pulse scarcely detectable, cold extremities, no reaction in pupils. Adrenalin into heart, camphor using method of Preobrazhensky, physiological solution intravenously.

26 *December*. Some improvement. Pulse 180, respiration 92, temperature 41. Camphor, nourishment via suppositories.

27 *December*. Pulse 152, respiration 50, temperature 39.8, reaction in pupils. Camphor subcutaneously.

28 *December*. Significant improvement. At noon sudden torrential sweat, temperature 37. Operation scars in former condition. Rebandaging. Appearance of appetite. Fluid nourishment.

29 *December*. Sudden discovery of loss of coat on forehead and sides of trunk. Called in for consultation: Professor Vasily Vasilyevich Bundarev of Department of Skin Diseases and Director of Moscow Model Veterinary Institute. Occurrence declared by them to be unrecorded in literature. Diagnosis remained unestablished. Temperature – normal.

Entry in pencil

In evening came first bark (8.15). Attention drawn by sharp change in timbre and tone (lowered). Instead of word 'woof-woof', bark in syllables 'a-o'. In tenor distantly reminiscent of groan.

30 December. Falling out of coat has assumed character of general loss of hair. Weighing produced unexpected result – weight 30 kg. on account of growth (elongation) of bones. Dog lying down as before.

31 December. Colossal appetite.

Blot in notebook. After blot in hurried handwriting:

At 12.12 in afternoon dog distinctly barked word: 'H–s–if'.

(*Break in notebook and subsequently, evidently by mistake because of agitation, is written*):

1 December. (*Crossed out, corrected.*)

1 January 1925. Photographed in morning. Distinctly barks 'Hsif', repeating this word loudly and seemingly joyfully. At 3 o'clock in afternoon (*in large letters*) laughed (?), causing maid Zina to faint. In evening pronounced 8 times in row word 'Hsif-etats', 'Hsif'.

In crooked letters in pencil:

Professor decoded word 'Hsif-etats', it means 'State fish'... Something monstr...

2 *January*. Photographed with magnesium flash while smiling. Got out of bed and stayed steady on hind legs half an hour. Almost my height.

Loose leaf in notebook:

Russian science almost suffered serious loss.

Professor Preobrazhensky's case history

At 1.13 Prof Preobrazhensky in deep faint. In falling hit head on chair leg. Valerian tincture.

In my and Zina's presence dog (if, of course, it can be called dog) had sworn at Prof Preobrazhensky with reference to his mother.

Break in entries.

6 *January*. (*Sometimes in pencil, sometimes in violet ink.*)

Today, after his tail dropped off, he pronounced quite distinctly the word 'pub'. Photographer working. The devil knows what's what.

* * *

I'm at a loss.

* * *

The professor's surgery curtailed. Starting at 5 p.m., from the consulting room where this creature is pacing, vulgar abuse can be clearly heard, and the words 'give us a couple more'.

7 January. He utters an awful lot of words: 'cab', 'no room', 'evening paper', 'ideal gift for children', and absolutely every word of abuse that there is in the Russian language.

His appearance is strange. His coat has remained only on the head, on the chin and on the chest. For the remainder he's bald, with flabby skin. In the area of the sex organs – a man in the making. The skull is increasing in size significantly. The forehead is sloping and low.

* * *

I swear to God, I'll go mad.

* * *

Philipp Philippovich still feels ill. I'm conducting most of the observations. (*Phonograph, photographs.*)

* * *

Rumours have spread around town.

* * *

Incalculable consequences. This afternoon the whole lane was full of these layabouts and old women. Idlers are still standing outside the windows even now. An amazing item appeared in the morning papers. 'Rumours about a Martian in Obukhov Lane have no foundation. They were spread by traders from the Sukharev Market and will be severely punished.' What Martian, damn it? It's just a nightmare.

* * *

Better still in the evening paper – they've written that a child's been born that plays the violin. And right there a picture – a violin and my photograph, and beneath it the caption: 'Prof Preobrazhensky, who performed a Caesarean section on the mother.' It's simply indescribable... A new word – 'policeman'.

* * *

It turns out Darya Petrovna was in love with me and nicked the photograph from P.P.'s album. After I'd sent the reporters away, one of them crept into the kitchen, etc.

* * *

The things going on during surgery hours! There were 82 calls today. The telephone's switched off. Childless ladies have gone mad and come...

* * *

The House Committee at full strength headed by Shvonder. Why – they don't know themselves.

8 January. Late in the evening a diagnosis was made. P.P., as a true scholar, admitted his mistake – the change of pituitary gland brings not rejuvenation, but complete humanisation (*underlined three times*). His astonishing, stunning discovery is not diminished by this at all.

He went for a walk around the apartment for the first time today. He laughed in the corridor, looking at the electric lamp. Then, accompanied by Philipp Philippovich and me, he proceeded into the study. He stands firm on his hind (*crossed out*)… on his feet and gives the impression of a small and poorly built man.

He laughed in the study. His smile is unpleasant and seems artificial. Then he scratched the back of his head, looked around, and I made a note of a new, distinctly pronounced phrase: 'bourgeois gits'. He swore. This swearing is methodical, continuous and, evidently, utterly meaningless. It has a somewhat phonographic character: as if this creature had heard words of abuse somewhere before, had automatically, subconsciously noted them in his brain, and now he's belching them out by the packet. But still, I'm not a psychiatrist, damn it.

For some reason the abuse makes an amazingly painful impression on Philipp Philippovich. There are moments when he abandons the restrained and cold observation of new phenomena and seems to lose patience. Thus at a moment of swearing he suddenly cried out fretfully:

'Stop it!!'

This had no effect.

After the walk in the study Sharik was installed by our combined efforts in the consulting room.

After that Philipp Philippovich and I had a conference. For the first time, I must confess, I saw this confident and incredibly intelligent man bewildered. Singing in his customary way, he asked: 'And so what are we going to do now?' And he himself replied, literally like this: 'The Moscow Seamstress, yes… "From Seville unto Granada." The Moscow Seamstress, dear Doctor…' I didn't understand at all. He explained: 'I'd like you please, Ivan Arnoldovich, to buy him linen, trousers and a jacket.'

9 January. His vocabulary is enriched every five minutes (on average) by a new word, and since this morning by phrases. It seems as if, frozen in his consciousness, they thaw out and emerge. The emerged word remains in use. Recorded by the phonograph since yesterday evening are: 'stop pushing', 'hit him', 'bastard', 'get off the footboard', 'I'll show you', 'America's recognition', 'primus'.

10 January. Dressing has taken place. He allowed the undershirt to be put on him willingly, even laughing cheerfully. He refused the long johns, expressing his protest in hoarse cries: 'Get in the queue, you sons of bitches, get in the queue!' He was dressed. The socks are too big for him.

In the notebook are some schematic drawings, by every indication depicting the transformation of a dog's leg into a human one.

Rear half of skeleton of foot (*Tarsus*) lengthens. Extension of toes. Nails.

Repeated systematic tuition in visiting lavatory. Servants utterly depressed. But the creature's ability to understand should be noted. The matter is proceeding perfectly well.

11 January. Completely reconciled to trousers, and uttered a long, jovial phrase, touching Philipp Philippovich's: 'Give us a cig – your trousers are too big.'

The coat on the head is thin and silky. Easily confused with hair. But coloured patches have remained on the crown of the head. Today the last of the down came off the ears. Colossal appetite. Ate herring with enthusiasm.

At 5 o'clock in the afternoon an event: for the first time the words uttered by the creature were not plucked from surrounding phenomena but were a reaction to them. Namely: when the professor ordered him: 'Don't throw leftovers on the floor,' he unexpectedly replied: 'Shove off, scumbag.'

P.P. was staggered, then collected himself and said:

'If you permit yourself to call me or the doctor names one more time, you'll be in trouble.'

I was photographing Sharik at the time. I guarantee he understood the professor's words. A sullen shadow lay on his face. He gave a look of some irritation from under his brows, but calmed down.

Hurrah, he understands!

12 January. Putting of hands in trouser pockets. We're breaking him of swearing. He whistled 'Oh, Little Apple'. Sustains conversation.

I can't resist a number of hypotheses: to hell with rejuvenation for the time being. Something else is immeasurably more important: Prof Preobrazhensky's astonishing experiment has revealed one of the secrets of the human brain. Henceforth the mysterious function of the pituitary gland – the cerebral appendage – is elucidated. It determines human character. Its hormones can be termed the most important in the organism – the hormones of character. A new field of science opens up: without any Faustian retort a homunculus has been created.[25] The surgeon's scalpel has summoned to life a new human individual. Prof Preobrazhensky, you are a creator. (*Blot.*)

But I've digressed... And so, he sustains conversation. In my assumption, this is how things stand: the now accepted pituitary gland has opened up the speech centre in the dog's brain, and words have poured out in a torrent. In my opinion, before us is a brain that has come to life, developed, and not a brain that is newly created. Oh, wondrous confirmation of evolutionary theory! Oh, immense chain from dog to Mendeleyev[26] the chemist! Another hypothesis of mine: Sharik's brain in the canine period of his life accumulated masses of concepts. All the words with which he began operating first and foremost are street words, he heard them and harboured them in his brain. Now, walking down the street, I look with secret horror at oncoming dogs. God knows what they've got hidden away in their brains.

* * *

Sharik could read. Read!!! (3 *exclamation marks*) I guessed it. From State Fish. Specifically, could read backwards. And I even know where the solution to this riddle lies: in the cross section of the dog's optic nerves.

* * *

The things going on in Moscow – they pass human understanding. Seven Sukharev traders are already in prison for spreading rumours about the end of the world, brought on by the Bolsheviks. Darya Petrovna was talking about it and even named the precise date: 28th November 1925, on the day of the sainted martyr Stephen, the earth will fly into the axis of the heavens... Some swindlers are already giving lectures. We've caused such a hullabaloo with this pituitary gland, it's enough to make you flee the apartment. I've moved to Preobrazhensky's at his request and spend the nights in the waiting room with Sharik. The consulting room has been turned into a waiting room. Shvonder has proved to be right. The House Committee is gloating. There's not a single pane of glass in the cabinets because of his jumping. We've barely managed to break him of it.

* * *

Something strange is happening to Philipp. When I told him about my hypotheses and hope of developing Sharik into a very elevated spiritual personality, he hemmed and replied: 'Do you think so?' His tone is ominous. Surely I'm not mistaken? The old man has thought of something. While I'm busy with the case history, he sits reading the history of the man from whom we took the pituitary gland.

* * *

Loose leaf in the notebook.

Klim Grigoryevich Chugunkin, 25 years, unmarried. Non-Party member, a sympathiser. On trial three times and acquitted: first time thanks to lack of evidence, second time his background saved him, third time – suspended sentence of 15 years' hard labour. Thefts. Profession – playing the balalaika in taverns.

Short, poorly built. Enlarged liver (alcohol). Cause of death – knife blow to the heart in The Stop Signal pub by the Preobrazhenskaya Gate.

* * *

The old man sits reading Klim's case history and can't tear himself away. I don't understand what the matter is. He muttered something about how he hadn't thought of examining the whole of Chugunkin's corpse in the morgue. What the matter is, I don't understand. Isn't it all the same whose pituitary gland it is?

17 January. Have made no notes for several days: been sick with influenza. During this time appearance has taken definitive shape.

a) absolutely human in composition of body;

b) weight around 50 kg.;

c) stature small;

d) head small;

e) has started smoking;

f) eats human food;

g) dresses independently;

h) conducts conversation fluently.

* * *

There's the pituitary gland for you! (*Blot.*)

* * *

With this I end the case history. Before us is a new organism; it needs to be observed from the beginning.

Appendix: shorthand records of speech, phonograph recordings, photographs.

Signature: assistant to Professor P.P. Preobrazhensky,

– Dr Bormental

6

It was a winter's evening. The end of January. The pre-prandial, pre-surgery hour. On the frame of the door into the waiting room hung a white sheet of paper, on which was written in Philipp Philippovich's hand:

> *'I forbid the eating of sunflower seeds in the apartment.*
> *   – P. Preobrazhensky.'*

– and in blue pencil, in letters large as fancy cakes, in Bormental's hand:

> *'The playing of musical instruments between 5 p.m. and 7 a.m. is forbidden.'*

Then in Zina's hand:

> *'When you come back, tell Philipp Philippovich: I don't know where he went. Fyodor said it was with Shvonder.'*

In Preobrazhensky's hand:

> *'Will I have to wait a hundred years for a glazier?'*

In Darya Petrovna's hand (printed):

> *'Zina's gone to the shop, said she'd bring him.'*

In the dining room the sense of evening was complete, thanks to a lamp under a cherry silk shade. The light falling from the sideboard was cut in two – the mirrored panes of glass were taped with a diagonal cross from one facet to the other. Philipp

Philippovich, bending over the table, was immersed in the huge sheet of a newspaper. Lightning strikes contorted his face, and through his teeth there sprinkled truncated, dock-tailed, grumbling words. He was reading an article:

'There is no doubt it is his illegitimate (as they used to say in rotten bourgeois society) son. That's how our pseudo-intellectual bourgeoisie amuses itself. Each one of them knows how to occupy seven rooms until the red ray of the shining sword of justice flashes above him.

Shv—r.'

Two rooms away, very insistently and with flashy dexterity, a balalaika was being played, and the sounds of the intricate variation 'Shines the Moonlight' blended in Philipp Philip-povich's head with the words of the article into a hateful stew. On finishing reading he spat dryly over his shoulder and began to sing mechanically through his teeth:

' "Shi-i-ines the moonlight... shines the moonlight... shines the moonlight..." Ugh, it's stuck in my head, that damned tune!'

He rang the bell. Zina's face poked in between the panels of the curtain.

'Tell him it's 5 o'clock and to stop, and call him in here, please.'

Philipp Philippovich sat by the table in an armchair. Between the fingers of his left hand protruded the brown stub of a cigar. By the curtain, leaning against the door frame with one leg behind the other, stood a man short in stature and unattractive in appearance. The hair on his head grew coarse, like bushes on a cleared field, while his face was covered in unshaven down. The forehead was striking for its lack of height. Almost immediately above the black paintbrushes of the far-flung eyebrows began the big thick brush of the head.

His jacket, torn under the left armpit, had straw scattered all over it, his striped trousers were ripped at the left knee and stained with lilac paint at the right. Knotted at the man's neck was a tie of a toxic sky-blue colour with a fake ruby tiepin. The colour of this tie was so garish that from time to time, closing his exhausted eyes, Philipp Philippovich could see in the total darkness – now on the ceiling, now on the wall – a flaming torch with a light blue corona. Opening them, he was blinded again, since lacquered shoes with white spats, spraying out fans of light, leapt into his eyes from the floor.

'As though wearing galoshes,' thought Philipp Philippovich with an unpleasant sensation, then sighed, started wheezing, and began to busy himself with the extinguished cigar. The man by the door cast occasional glances at the professor with his rather lacklustre eyes and smoked a cigarette, scattering ash on his cuff.

The clock on the wall alongside the wooden hazel grouse rang five times. Something was still groaning inside it when Philipp Philippovich entered into conversation.

'I think I've asked you twice already not to sleep on the sleeping-bench in the kitchen – particularly not in the daytime?'

The man coughed huskily, as though he had choked on a fruit-stone, and replied:

'The air's nicer in the kitchen.'

His voice was unusual, rather muffled and at the same time booming, as if in a little barrel.

Philipp Philippovich shook his head and asked:

'Where did that disgusting thing come from? I'm talking about the tie.'

The man, following the finger with his eyes, used them to squint over the top of his pouting lip and looked lovingly at the tie.

'What's "disgusting" about it?' he began, 'it's a very smart tie. Darya Petrovna gave it me.'

'Darya Petrovna gave you an abomination, like those shoes. What is that shiny rubbish? Where are they from? What did I request? Buy some de-cent shoes; and what are they? Surely Dr Bormental didn't choose ones like that?'

'I had him get lacquer ones. What, aren't I as good as every-one else? Go to Kuznetsky[27] – everyone's wearing lacquered ones.'

Philipp Philippovich gave his head a shake and began weightily:

'Sleeping on the sleeping-bench must stop. Is that under-stood? What effrontery! You're in the way, you know. There are women there.'

The man's face darkened and his lips pouted.

'Well, women indeed. Just think. What fine ladies. Just or-dinary servants, but with the swank of a commissar. This is all that Zinka[28] telling tales.'

Philipp Philippovich threw him a stern glance:

'Don't you dare call Zina "Zinka"! Is that understood?'

Silence.

'Is that understood, I'm asking you?'

'Yes.'

'Get that muck off of your neck. Please… just you… you take a look at yourself in the mirror, what do you look like? Some sort of fairground joke. No throwing cigarette-ends on the floor – that's the umpteenth time I've told you. I don't want to hear one more obscenity in the apartment! Don't spit! There's the spittoon. Take care with the urinal. Stop all these conversations with Zina. She's complaining that you're stalking her in the dark. Watch out! Who answered a patient "the devil only knows"? Really, are you in some low dive, or something?'

'You're really giving me a hard time, Dad,' the man suddenly pronounced piteously.

Philipp Philippovich reddened, his spectacles flashed.

'Who is it here that's your "dad"? What sort of familiarity is this? I don't want to hear that word any more! Call me by my name and patronymic!'

An impudent expression began to burn in the man.

'Why is it you're always... First it's "don't spit", then "don't smoke". "Don't go there..." What is all this at the end of the day? It's just like in a tram. Why won't you let me live?! And as for "dad" – you're being unfair there. Did I ask to have an operation done?' the man barked in indignation. 'A very pretty business! Grabbed an animal, cut its head into strips with a knife, and now they look down their noses. P'raps I didn't give my permission for the operation. And neither,' (the man raised his eyes to the ceiling, as though recalling some formulation) 'and neither did my relatives. P'raps I'm within my rights to sue.'

Philipp Philippovich's eyes became perfectly round, the cigar tumbled out of his hands. 'Well, what a sort,' flew through his mind.

'What's this, sir,' he asked, narrowing his eyes, 'are you so good as to be unhappy about being turned into a man? Perhaps you'd prefer to be running around the rubbish tips again? Freezing in gateways? Well, if I'd known!...'

'What are you always criticising for – rubbish tip, rubbish tip. I was getting my daily crust. And what if I'd died under your knife? What do you have to say on that score, Comrade?'

'"Philipp Philippovich"!' exclaimed Philipp Philippovich in irritation, 'I'm not your comrade! It's monstrous!' – 'It's a nightmare, a nightmare,' he thought.

'Oh well of course, yes...' began the man ironically, and stuck a leg out triumphantly, 'we understand, sir. What kind of comrades are we for you? How could we be? We haven't been to universities, haven't lived in fifteen-room apartments with bathrooms. Only it's about time to stop all that now. Nowadays everyone has his rights...'

Philipp Philippovich, turning pale, listened to the man's arguments. The latter interrupted his speech and moved demonstratively towards the ashtray with his chewed-up cigarette in his hand. His gait was sauntering. He spent a long time crushing the stub in the bowl with an expression that clearly said: 'There! There!' Having extinguished the cigarette, he suddenly snapped his teeth in mid-stride and buried his nose in his armpit.

'Catch the fleas with your fingers! With your fingers!' cried Philipp Philippovich furiously, 'and I don't understand, where is it you get them from?'

'What, breed them or something, do I?' said the man, offended, 'the fleas must like me,' at this point he fumbled about with his fingers in the lining in the sleeve and released into the air a tuft of ginger-coloured cotton wool.

Philipp Philippovich turned his gaze towards the garlands on the ceiling and began drumming his fingers on the table. The man, having executed the flea, walked away and sat down on a chair. In so doing, dropping his wrists, he hung his arms down parallel to the lapels of his jacket. His eyes looked side-long towards the wooden blocks of the parquet. He was contemplating his shoes, and this was giving him great pleasure. Philipp Philippovich looked to where harsh spots of light shone on the blunt toes, narrowed his eyes and began:

'What other matter did you want to inform me of?'

'Ah yes, the matter! A simple matter. I need documents, Philipp Philippovich.'

Philipp Philippovich was a little perturbed.

'Hm... Damn it! Documents! Really... Hm... but perhaps one could somehow manage without?...' his voice sounded uncertain and mournful.

'Please,' replied the man confidently, 'how can you be without documents? It's simply – excuse me. You know for yourself, a man without documents is strictly forbidden to exist. Firstly, the House Committee…'

'What does the House Committee have to do with it?'

'What do you mean, what does it have to do with it? They meet me and they ask – when, they say, esteemed sir, are you going to register?'

'Oh, Good Lord,' exclaimed Philipp Philippovich despondently, ' "they meet you and they ask"… I can imagine what you say to them. And I've forbidden you, you know, to slouch about on the stairs.'

'What am I, a convict?' said the man in surprise, and his consciousness of his rectitude began to burn even in the ruby. 'And what do you mean, "slouch about"?! Your words are quite offensive. I walk like everyone does.'

At this he shuffled his lacquered feet across the parquet.

Philipp Philippovich fell silent, his eyes went off to one side. 'Still, I must restrain myself,' he thought. Going up to the sideboard, he drank down a glass of water in one go.

'Excellent, sir,' he began a little more calmly, 'it's not the words that matter. So, what does this delightful House Committee of yours say?'

'What can it say… And you've no reason to go branding it as "delightful". It defends interests.'

'Whose interests, permit me to enquire?'

'It's obvious whose – the working element.'

Philipp Philippovich opened his eyes wide.

'And how is it you're a worker?'

'Well it's obvious I'm not a Nepman[29].'

'Well, all right. So what does it actually need in the defence of your revolutionary interest?'

'Obviously, to register me. Where's it heard of, they say, for a man to live in Moscow unregistered? That's one thing. And the main thing is a record card. I don't want to be a deserter. And then again – a trade union, the labour exchange…'

'Permit me to learn on what basis I'm to register you? On the basis of this tablecloth or of my own passport? I mean, it is, after all, necessary to take account of the situation. Don't forget that you… er… hm… I mean, you are, so to speak – a creature that has appeared unexpectedly, a creature of the laboratory.' Philipp Philippovich spoke more and more uncertainly.

The man was triumphantly silent.

'Excellent, sir. Well then, so at the end of it all you need to be registered, and everything in general needs to be arranged according to the plan of this House Committee of yours? But you don't have either a name or a surname, you know.'

'You're wrong there. I can choose myself a name perfectly easily. I get it printed in the paper, and there you go.'

'And how do you wish to be known?'

The man adjusted his tie and replied:

'Polygraph Polygraphovich.'

'Don't play the fool,' responded Philipp Philippovich glumly, 'I'm talking to you seriously.'

A sarcastic smirk contorted the man's little moustache.

'There's something I can't understand,' he began cheerfully and sensibly. 'I mustn't eff and blind. I mustn't spit. But all I hear from you is: "Fool, fool." Clearly, only professors are allowed to curse in the R.S.F.S.R.[30]'

Philipp Philippovich became bloodshot and, in filling up a glass, broke it. After having a drink out of another one, he thought: 'A little longer, and he'll start lecturing me, and he'll be absolutely right. I can no longer keep myself under control.'

He turned on the chair, inclined his torso with exaggerated politeness and with iron firmness pronounced:

'Ex-cuse me. My nerves are upset. Your name seemed strange to me. Where, I wonder, did you dig one like that up for yourself?'

'The House Committee advised me. Looked in the calendar – what do you want, they said? And so I chose.'

'There can't be anything of the sort in any calendar.[31]'

'That's quite surprising,' the man smirked, 'when it's hanging in your consulting room.'

Without getting up, Philipp Philippovich leant back towards the button on the wallpaper, and Zina appeared at the sound of the bell.

'The calendar from the consulting room.'

A pause elapsed. When Zina returned with the calendar, Philipp Philippovich asked:

'Where?'

'It's celebrated on the 4th of March.'

'Show me... Hm... Damn it... Into the stove with it, Zina, straight away.'

Zina, her eyes popping out in fright, went away with the calendar, while the man shook his head reproachfully.

'Permit me to learn your surname?'

'I'm prepared to take a hereditary surname.'

'What's that? Hereditary? Namely?'

'Sharikov.'

* * *

Before the desk in the study stood the Chairman of the House Committee, Shvonder, wearing a double-breasted leather jacket. Dr Bormental sat in an armchair. As he did so, on the doctor's cheeks, which were rosy from the frost (he had only just returned), there was just as bewildered an expression as Philipp Philippovich wore, sitting alongside him.

'So how am I to write it?' he asked impatiently.

'Well,' began Shvonder, 'it's no complicated matter. Write an attestation, Citizen Professor. That, you know, it's like this, the bearer hereof is truly Sharikov, Polygraph Polygraphovich, hm... generated in your, you know, apartment.'

Bormental shifted in puzzlement in the armchair. Philipp Philippovich tugged at his whiskers.

'Hm... Damn it all! You can't possibly imagine anything more silly. He wasn't generated at all, but simply... well, in a word...'

'That's your affair,' pronounced Shvonder, quietly gloating, 'whether he was generated or not... The long and the short of it is, you were doing an experiment, Professor, weren't you?! And you created Citizen Sharikov.'

'And it's perfectly simple,' barked Sharikov from the book-case. He was peering at the tie, reflected in the mirrored abyss.

'I would ask you,' snapped Philipp Philippovich, 'to keep out of the conversation. You're wrong to say "and it's perfectly simple" – it's not simple at all.'

'How can I keep out of it?' Sharikov started grumbling touchily.

Shvonder supported him at once.

'Forgive me, Professor, Citizen Sharikov is absolutely right. It's his right to participate in the discussion of his own fate, particularly inasmuch as the matter concerns documents. Documents are the most important thing in the world.'

At this moment a deafening peal right in the ear interrupted the conversation. Philipp Philippovich spoke into the receiver: 'Yes!', then reddened and shouted:

'Please don't disturb me with trifles. What business is it of yours?' And he thrust the receiver forcefully back into its holder.

Idyllic delight spread over Shvonder's face. Turning crimson, Philipp Philippovich cried:

'In short, let's get this finished.'

He tore a sheet from a notepad and jotted down a few words, then irritably read out loud:

'"I hereby attest..." The devil knows what's going on... Hm... "The bearer hereof, a man produced in a laboratory experiment by means of an operation on the brain, requires documents..." Damn it! I'm completely against getting these idiotic documents. Signature – "Professor Preobrazhensky".'

'It's rather strange, Professor,' said Shvonder, offended. 'How can you call documents idiotic? I can't allow the residence of an undocumented lodger in the building, and one not registered with the police for military service, what's more. What if there's a war with the imperialist predators?'

'I'm not going fighting anywhere!' Sharikov suddenly yapped gloomily into the bookcase.

Shvonder was dumbstruck, but quickly recovered and re-marked to Sharikov courteously:

'Citizen Sharikov, you're talking in a manner that's socially irresponsible in the highest degree. It's essential to be registered for military service.'

'I'll get registered, but as for fighting – not bloody likely,' replied Sharikov antagonistically, adjusting his knot.

It was Shvonder's turn to be confused. Preobrazhensky threw a malicious and melancholy glance at Bormental: 'How's that for morality?' Bormental gave a meaningful nod of the head.

'I'm seriously wounded, from the operation,' whined Sharikov gloomily, 'see what a finish they've given me,' and he pointed to his head. Across the forehead stretched a very fresh operation scar.

'Are you an anarchistic individualist?' asked Shvonder, rais-ing his brows high.

'I'm due a white ticket[32],' replied Sharikov to this.

'Well, all right, it's not important just now,' replied the surprised Shvonder, 'the point is, we'll send the professor's attestation off to the police and you'll have documents issued to you.'

'There's this, er…' Philipp Philippovich suddenly interrupted him, evidently tormented by some particular thought, 'do you have a free room in the building? I'm prepared to buy it.'

Little yellow sparks appeared in Shvonder's brown eyes.

'No, Professor, to my very great regret. Nor is one expected.'

Philipp Philippovich pursed his lips and said nothing. Again the telephone pealed out like one possessed. Philipp Philippovich, without asking anything, silently threw the receiver out of its holder so that, after spinning around for a while, it hung down on its blue flex. Everyone gave a start. 'The old man's got himself worked up,' thought Bormental, while Shvonder, with his eyes flashing, bowed and left the room.

Sharikov, with his welted boots squeaking, set off after him.

The professor remained alone with Bormental. After a short silence Philipp Philippovich gave his head a little shake and began to speak:

'Honestly, it's a nightmare. Don't you see? I swear to you, my dear Doctor, I'm more worn out after these two weeks than over the last fourteen years! What an awful sort, I'm telling you…'

In the distance there was a muffled cracking of glass, then a woman's stifled scream flew up and immediately died away. A devilish force whacked along the wallpaper in the corridor, heading towards the consulting room, there was a crash of some sort there, and it instantly flew back past again. Doors slammed, and in response from the kitchen came Darya Petrovna's low cry. Then Sharikov began howling.

'My God, something else!' shouted Philipp Philippovich, rushing to the doors.

'A cat,' realised Bormental, and leapt out after him. They sped down the corridor into the entrance hall, burst into it, from there turned into the corridor to the lavatory and the bathroom. Zina leapt out from the kitchen and bumped right into Philipp Philippovich.

'How many times have I given the order that there should be no cats,' shouted Philipp Philippovich in fury. 'Where is he?! Ivan Arnoldovich, for God's sake, calm the patients in the waiting room!'

'In the bathroom, the confounded devil's sitting in the bathroom,' Zina shouted breathlessly.

Philipp Philippovich put all his weight against the bathroom door, but it did not yield.

'Open up this instant!'

In reply, something in the locked bathroom started jumping around the walls, basins tumbled down, and Sharikov's wild voice roared indistinctly behind the door:

'I'll kill you on the spot...'

Water began gurgling in the pipes and pouring out. Philipp Philippovich leant on the door and started tearing at it. A sweating Darya Petrovna, her face contorted, appeared on the threshold of the kitchen. Then the transom that looked out from the bathroom into the kitchen just below ceiling level cracked in a jagged crack, and out of it fell two pieces of glass, and after them tumbled a tiger-striped cat of the most immense size with a blue ribbon on its neck, looking like a policeman. It fell straight onto the table into a long dish, breaking it lengthways, and from the table onto the floor, then it turned around on three legs, while it waved the right one as if in a dance, and immediately slipped out through a narrow crack onto the back staircase. The crack widened, and the cat was replaced by the physiognomy of an old woman in a headscarf. The old woman's skirt, covered in white dots, appeared in the kitchen. The old woman wiped her sunken mouth with an index finger and thumb, surveyed the kitchen with slightly swollen and prickly eyes and pronounced with curiosity:

'O Lord Jesus!'

A pale Philipp Philippovich crossed the kitchen and asked the old woman sternly:

'What do you want?'

'I'd be curious to have a look at the talking dog,' replied the old woman ingratiatingly and crossed herself.

Philipp Philippovich grew still paler, went right up to the old woman and whispered chokingly:

'Out of the kitchen this instant!'

The old woman backed away towards the doors and, offended, began:

'That really is ever so rude, Mr Professor.'

'Out, I say!' Philipp Philippovich repeated, and his eyes became round as an owl's. He personally slammed the back door behind the old woman. 'Darya Petrovna, I did ask you!'

'Philipp Philippovich,' replied Darya Petrovna in despair, squeezing her bared hands into fists, 'what can I do? Folks are forcing their way in all day long, even if I drop everything.'

The water in the bathroom roared indistinctly and menacingly, but the voice was no longer audible. In came Dr Bormental.

'Ivan Arnoldovich, I earnestly request you... hm... How many patients are there?'

'Eleven,' replied Bormental.

'Send them all away, I'm not seeing anyone today.'

Philipp Philippovich rapped his knuckle on the door and cried:

'Be so good as to come out this minute! Why have you locked yourself in?'

'Bow-wow!' replied Sharikov's plaintive and flat voice.

'What the devil!... I can't hear, turn off the water.'

'Woof! Woof!...'

'Turn off the water, will you! What's he done – I don't understand...' exclaimed Philipp Philippovich, flying into a rage.

Zina and Darya Petrovna, open-mouthed, looked at the door in despair. To the noise of the water had been added a suspicious splashing. Philipp Philippovich once again drummed his fist on the door.

'There he is!' Darya Petrovna cried out from the kitchen.

Philipp Philippovich dashed in. In the broken window just below the ceiling Polygraph Polygraphovich's physiognomy had appeared and poked itself into the kitchen. It was twisted, the eyes were tearful, and a scratch stretched the length of the nose, blazing with fresh blood.

'Have you gone mad?' asked Philipp Philippovich. 'Why won't you come out?'

Even Sharikov himself glanced back in anguish and terror and replied:

'I've locked myself in.'

'Unlock it. What, have you never seen a lock before?'

'It won't unlock, though, damn it!' replied Polygraph in fright.

'Heavens! He's put the safety catch on!' exclaimed Zina, and clapped her hands together.

'There's this little button there!' Philipp Philippovich cried out, trying to make himself heard above the noise of the water, 'press it downwards... Go on, press it down! Down!'

Sharikov vanished, and a minute later appeared in the window once more.

'I can't see a damn thing,' he barked through the window in horror.

'Turn on the light then. – He's gone mad!'

'That ruddy great tomcat smashed the light,' replied Sharikov, 'and I tried to grab him by the legs, the bastard, and I pulled the tap off, and now I can't find it.'

All three clapped their hands together, and in that position they froze.

Some five minutes later Bormental, Zina and Darya Petrovna were sitting beside one another at the foot of the door on a wet, rolled-up rug, pressing it with their rear portions to the gap under the door, while the doorman Fyodor was climbing up a wooden stepladder into the transom with Darya Petrovna's lighted wedding candle. His backside, wearing large grey checks, appeared fleetingly in the air and then disappeared in the aperture.

'Yow... bow-wow!' Sharikov somehow cried through the roar of the water.

Under pressure it splashed several times from the transom onto the kitchen ceiling, then the water stopped.

Fyodor's voice was heard:

'Philipp Philippovich, we've got to open up anyway, let it spread out, we'll suck it up out of the kitchen.'

'Open up then!' cried Philipp Philippovich angrily.

The trio rose from the rug, the door from the bathroom was given a push, and at once a wave gushed into the little corridor. There it divided into three streams: straight ahead – into the lavatory opposite, to the right – into the kitchen, and to the left – into the entrance hall. Sloshing and jumping, Zina slammed the door into the entrance hall. Ankle-deep in water, Fyodor came out smiling for some reason. He was all wet, and looked as if he were wearing oilcloth.

'It was all I could do to plug it, the pressure's high,' he elucidated.

'Where is he?' asked Philipp Philippovich, and with a curse raised one foot.

'He's afraid to come out,' explained Fyodor with a silly grin.

'You're going to beat me, Dad,' came Sharikov's tearful voice from the bathroom.

'Halfwit!' responded Philipp Philippovich curtly.

Zina and Darya Petrovna, with their skirts tucked up to their knees and with bare legs, and Sharikov and the doorman, barefooted and with their trousers rolled up, were hurling wet cloths around the kitchen floor and wringing them out into dirty buckets and the sink. The neglected stove was humming. Water was draining away through the door onto the echoing stairs, right into the stairwell, and falling into the basement.

Bormental, stretched up on tiptoe, was standing in a deep puddle on the parquet in the entrance hall and was conducting negotiations through the door, which was slightly ajar and on the chain.

'There'll be no surgery today, the professor's unwell. Be so kind as to move away from the door, we have a burst pipe.'

'So when is there a surgery?' a voice outside the door tried to ascertain, 'I'd only need a moment…'

'I can't help,' Bormental shifted from the toes of his shoes to the heels, 'the professor's in bed and the pipe's burst. Tomorrow, please. Zina, dear! Wipe away from here, or else it'll pour out onto the main staircase.'

'The cloths aren't working.'

'We'll bail out with mugs in a minute,' responded Fyodor, 'in just a minute.'

One ring at the door followed another, and Bormental already stood with the entire sole of his shoe in the water.

'When will the operation be?' a voice kept badgering, and tried to force its way into the crack.

'A pipe's burst…'

'I could get through in galoshes…'

Bluish silhouettes appeared outside the door.

'It's not possible, tomorrow, please.'

'But I have an appointment.'

'Tomorrow. An accident with the water-pipe.'

At the doctor's feet Fyodor was wriggling in a lake, scraping away with a mug, while Sharikov, covered in scratches, had thought of a new method. He rolled up a huge cloth, lay down on his stomach in the water and pushed it back from the entrance hall into the lavatory.

'What are you pushing it all over the apartment for, you devil?' Darya Petrovna raged, 'pour it into the sink.'

'What's the sink got to do with it?' replied Sharikov, trying to catch the murky water in his hands, 'it'll get out onto the main stairs.'

A little bench rolled out from the corridor with a gnashing sound, and stretched up on it, balancing, was Philipp Philippovich in blue striped socks.

'Ivan Arnoldovich, stop answering the door. Go into the bedroom, I'll give you a pair of slippers.'

'It's all right, Philipp Philippovich, it's no problem.'

'Put galoshes on.'

'No, it's all right. My feet are already wet anyway.'

'Oh, my God!' said Philipp Philippovich, upset.

'What a pesky animal!' Sharikov suddenly commented, and rode out on his haunches with a soup bowl in his hand.

Bormental slammed the door, could not contain himself and burst out laughing. Philipp Philippovich's nostrils flared, his spectacles flashed.

'Of whom are you speaking?' he asked of Sharikov from on high. 'Permit me to learn.'

'I'm speaking of the cat. Such a scumbag,' replied Sharikov, his eyes darting about.

'You know, Sharikov,' responded Philipp Philippovich, taking breath, 'I have positively never seen a more impudent creature than you.'

Bormental tittered.

'You,' Philipp Philippovich continued, 'are simply insolent.

How do you dare to say that? You are the cause of all this, and still permit... No! It's the devil knows what!'

'Sharikov, tell me, please,' began Bormental, 'how much longer are you going to go chasing after cats? Shame on you! It's a disgrace, you know! You savage!'

'Why am I a savage?' responded Sharikov sullenly. 'I'm no savage at all. You can't put up with him in the apartment. All he does is look for a way of thieving something. He scoffed Darya's mince. I wanted to teach him a lesson.'

'You should be taught a lesson yourself!' replied Philipp Philippovich, 'you take a look at your physiognomy in the mirror.'

'Almost took my eye out,' responded Sharikov gloomily, touching the eye with a wet, dirty hand.

When the parquet, black with moisture, had dried out a little, all the mirrors were covered in a film like in a bathhouse and the ringing had ceased, Philipp Philippovich stood in the entrance hall in red morocco-leather slippers.

'This is for you, Fyodor.'

'I'm most humbly grateful.'

'Get changed straight away. And you know what: have some of Darya Petrovna's vodka.'

'I'm most humbly grateful.' Fyodor dithered a moment, then said: 'There's something else, Philipp Philippovich. I'm sorry, I really do feel ashamed. Only – for the glass in apartment number seven... Citizen Sharikov was chucking stones...'

'At a cat?' asked Philipp Philippovich, growing gloomy as a cloud.

'That's just it, at the owner of the apartment. He's already been threatening to take it to court.'

'Damn!'

'Sharikov gave their cook a cuddle, and he set about chasing him off. Well, and they had a row.'

'For God's sake, always inform me of such things straight away! How much is needed?'

'One and a half.'

Philipp Philippovich drew out three shiny fifty-kopek pieces and handed them to Fyodor.

'And then you have to pay a rouble and a half on account of that swine as well,' a muffled voice was heard in the doorway, 'while he himself...'

Philipp Philippovich turned, bit his lip and silently leant on Sharikov, forced him out into the waiting room and locked him in. Sharikov immediately began drumming his fists on the door from within.

'Don't you dare!' exclaimed Philipp Philippovich in an obviously sick voice.

'Well, that really is something,' remarked Fyodor meaningfully, 'I've not seen such an insolent one in all my life.'

Bormental rose up as if from out of the ground.

'Philipp Philippovich, please, don't worry.'

The energetic Aesculapius[33] unlocked the door into the waiting room and from there came his voice:

'What's this? Are you in a tavern, or something?'

'That's right,' added Fyodor decisively, 'that's just right... And a clip across the ear too...'

'Oh, come now, Fyodor,' muttered Philipp Philippovich sadly.

'Forgive me, but I feel sorry for you, Philipp Philippovich.'

7

'No, no, no!' began Bormental insistently, 'be so good as to tuck it in.'

'What's the matter... honest to God,' Sharikov started grumbling discontentedly.

'I'm grateful to you, Doctor,' said Philipp Philippovich affectionately, 'because I'm already tired of giving reprimands.'

'All the same, I won't let you eat until you've tucked it in. Zina, take the mayonnaise away from Sharikov.'

'What's all this "take it away",' said Sharikov, upset, 'I'll tuck it in at once.'

With his left hand he shielded the dish from Zina, and with his right he stuffed the napkin inside his collar and ended up looking like a customer at the hairdresser's.

'And use the fork, please,' added Bormental.

Sharikov gave a long sigh and began trying to catch pieces of sturgeon in their thick sauce.

'I'll have some more vodka?' he declared interrogatively.

'Won't that be enough for you?' enquired Bormental. 'You've been hitting the vodka too much of late.'

'Do you begrudge it?' enquired Sharikov with a look from under his brows.

'You're talking nonsense...' intervened a stern Philipp Philippovich, but Bormental interrupted him.

'Don't worry, Philipp Philippovich, I'll deal with this myself. You, Sharikov, are talking rubbish, and most exasperating of all is the fact that you talk it categorically and confidently. Of course I don't begrudge the vodka, especially as it's not even mine, but Philipp Philippovich's. Simply – it's harmful. That's the first thing, and the second is that even without vodka you behave improperly.'

Bormental indicated the repaired sideboard.

'Zinusha, give me some more fish, please,' said the professor.

Sharikov meanwhile had reached out for the carafe and, looking askance at Bormental, poured himself a glass.

'You should offer it to others too,' said Bormental, 'and like this: first to Philipp Philippovich, then to me, and in conclusion to yourself.'

A scarcely discernible satirical smile touched Sharikov's mouth, and he poured vodka into the glasses.

'You know, we do everything as if on parade,' he began, 'napkin here, tie there, and "excuse me" and "please – *merci*", but having it like in the real world – oh no, not that. You give yourselves a hard time like under the tsarist regime.'

'And how is it "in the real world"? – permit me to enquire.'

Sharikov gave Philipp Philippovich no reply to this, but raised his glass and pronounced:

'Well, I hope all...'

'And the same to you,' responded Bormental with a certain irony.

Sharikov splashed the contents of the glass out into his gullet, pulled a face, brought a little piece of bread up to his nose, sniffed, and then swallowed, at which his eyes filled with tears.

'Length of time,' Philipp Philippovich suddenly said, abruptly and as if distractedly.

Bormental cast a sidelong look of surprise at him.

'I'm sorry...'

'Length of time!' Philipp Philippovich repeated and shook his head bitterly, 'there's nothing you can do about it – Klim.'

Bormental peered sharply and with extreme interest into Philipp Philippovich's eyes.

'Do you suppose so, Philipp Philippovich?'

'There's no supposing, I'm certain of it.'

'Surely...' Bormental started, then stopped with a sidelong glance at Sharikov.

The latter frowned suspiciously.

'*Später*[34],' said Philipp Philippovich quietly.

'*Gut*[35],' responded his assistant.

Zina brought in a turkey. Bormental poured Philipp Philippovich some red wine and offered it to Sharikov.

'I don't want any. I'll have some vodka instead.' His face became oily, sweat stood out on his forehead, he got merry. Philipp Philippovich grew somewhat kinder too after the wine. His eyes brightened, and he glanced more favourably at Sharikov, whose black head sat in the napkin like a fly in sour cream.

But Bormental, after fortifying himself, displayed an inclination for activity.

'Well, sir, what shall you and I undertake this evening?' he enquired of Sharikov.

The latter blinked a while and replied:

'Best of all, let's go to the circus.'

'Every day to the circus,' remarked Philipp Philippovich good-humouredly, 'that's rather boring in my view. In your place I'd go to the theatre once at least.'

'I'm not going to the theatre,' responded Sharikov antagonistically and crossed himself in front of his mouth.

'Hiccoughing at the table ruins other people's appetites,' Bormental declared mechanically. 'You'll forgive me... Why is it exactly you don't like the theatre?'

Sharikov looked into his empty glass as if through binoculars, had a think and stuck his lips out.

'It's playing the fool... They talk and talk... Just counter-revolution.'

Philipp Philippovich leant back in his Gothic chair and began chuckling so, the gold palisade in his mouth started sparkling. Bormental only turned his head back and forth.

'You should read something,' he suggested, 'or else, you know...'

'I do read as it is, I do,' replied Sharikov, then all of a sudden he greedily and quickly poured himself half a tumbler of vodka.

'Zina,' cried Philipp Philippovich in alarm, 'take the vodka away, child. It's no longer needed. And what is it you read?'

A picture suddenly flashed through his head: an uninhabited island, a palm tree, a man in an animal skin and a pointed hat. 'Robinson[36] will be good...'.

'That... What's it called... Engels' correspondence with that... what's his name, the devil? – Kautsky[37].'

Bormental stopped his fork with its piece of white meat halfway to his mouth, while Philipp Philippovich spilt his wine. Sharikov at that moment contrived to down the vodka.

Philipp Philippovich put his elbows on the table, peered at Sharikov and asked:

'Permit me to learn, what can you say regarding what you've read?'

Sharikov shrugged his shoulders.

'Well, I don't agree.'

'With whom? With Engels or Kautsky?'

'With either,' replied Sharikov.

'This is remarkable, I swear to God. "All who tell me that another..." And what could you for your part propose?'

'Well what can you propose?... They just write and write... a congress, some Germans or other... Your head swells up. Take everything and share it out...'

'That's what I thought,' exclaimed Philipp Philippovich, slapping his palm on the tablecloth, 'that is precisely what I supposed.'

'Do you know a method too?' asked Bormental, interested.

'What method do you need?' explained Sharikov, becoming talkative after the vodka, 'there's no trick to it. Because how can it be: one man's settled in seven rooms, he's got forty pairs of trousers, while another wanders around and looks for nutrition in rubbish bins.'

'Regarding seven rooms – it's to me, of course, you're alluding?' asked Philipp Philippovich, narrowing his eyes haughtily.

Sharikov shrank down and remained silent.

'Well then, all right, I'm not against sharing. Doctor, how many people did you turn away yesterday?'

'Thirty-nine,' replied Bormental immediately.

'Hm... 390 roubles. The three men bear the brunt. We won't count the ladies – Zina and Darya Petrovna. You, Sharikov, owe 130 roubles. Be so kind as to pay up.'

'This is a pretty business,' replied Sharikov in fright. 'What's that for?'

'For the tap and the cat,' Philipp Philippovich suddenly roared, emerging from his state of ironic calm.

'Philipp Philippovich,' exclaimed Bormental in alarm.

'Wait. For the outrage of which you were the cause, and thanks to which surgery hours were curtailed. It's quite intolerable. A man leaps all around the apartment like a Neanderthal, tearing off taps. Who killed Madame Polasukher's cat? Who...'

'Two days ago, Sharikov, you bit a lady on the stairs,' Bormental flew in.

'You stand...' growled Philipp Philippovich.

'But she'd slapped me across the face,' yelped Sharikov. 'My face isn't state property!'

'Because you'd pinched her on the breast,' shouted Bormental, overturning his glass. 'You stand...'

'You stand on the very lowest rung of development,' Philipp Philippovich drowned him out, 'you are a creature still only taking shape, weak with regard to intellect, all your actions are purely those of a wild animal, and you, in the presence of two men of university education, allow yourself with undue and utterly intolerable freedom to offer various words of advice on a cosmic scale and of cosmic stupidity about how to share everything out... while at the same time you've gulped down quantities of tooth powder...'

'Two days ago,' Bormental confirmed.

'Well then, sir,' thundered Philipp Philippovich, 'take note that you need to keep your nose clean – incidentally, why have you rubbed the zinc cream off it? – keep quiet and listen to what you're told. To learn, and try to become at least to some extent an acceptable member of the social group. Incidentally, what wretch provided you with that book?'

'Everyone's a wretch according to you,' replied Sharikov in fright, stunned by the attack from two sides.

'I can guess,' exclaimed Philipp Philippovich, flushing angrily.

'Well, then. Well, Shvonder gave me it. He's not a wretch... So I develop...'

'I can see how you're developing after Kautsky,' cried Philipp Philippovich shrilly and turning yellow. At this point he pressed furiously on the button in the wall. 'Today's incident demonstrates it better than anything. Zina!'

'Zina!' cried Bormental.

'Zina!' yelled the frightened Sharikov.

The pale Zina came running.

'Zina, in the waiting room... Is it in the waiting room?'

'It is,' replied Sharikov submissively, 'as green as vitriol.'

'A green book...'

'So now it's into the fire!' exclaimed Sharikov despairingly. 'It's state property, from a library!'

'The correspondence, it's called, of – what's his name – Engels and that devil... Into the stove with it!'

Zina flew off.

'I'd hang that Shvonder, honestly I would, from the nearest branch,' exclaimed Philipp Philippovich, biting fiercely into a turkey wing. 'He sits in this house, unbelievable scum that he is, like a boil. Not only does he write all sorts of senseless libels in the newspapers…'

Sharikov began casting malicious and ironic sidelong glances at the professor. Philipp Philippovich in his turn directed a sidelong glance towards him and fell silent.

'Oh, it doesn't seem there'll be anything good emerging in our apartment,' Bormental had the sudden prophetic thought.

On a round dish Zina brought in a baba that was ginger on the right side and rosy on the left and a coffee pot.

'I'm not going to eat it,' declared Sharikov immediately in a threateningly antagonistic way.

'Nobody's asking you to. Behave yourself properly. Doctor, please.'

Dinner ended in silence.

Sharikov pulled a bent cigarette from his pocket and started giving off smoke. After finishing his coffee, Philipp Philippovich glanced at his watch, pressed the repeater button, and it gently chimed a quarter-past eight. Philipp Philippovich leant back in his customary way in his Gothic chair and reached for the newspaper on a side table.

'Doctor, will you go to the circus with him, please? Only for God's sake look in the programme to see there are no cats.'

'How is it they let such riff-raff into the circus?' remarked Sharikov sullenly, shaking his head.

'Well, they let all sorts in,' Philipp Philippovich responded ambiguously. 'What have they got on?'

'Solomonsky,' Bormental began reading out, 'has The Four something or others… Yussems, and The Dead Centre Man.'[38]

'What are these Yussems?' enquired Philipp Philippovich suspiciously.

'God knows. It's the first time I've come across the word.'

'Well then, better look at Nikitin's. It's essential everything should be clear.'

'At Nikitin's... Nikitin's... hm... elephants, and The Limit of Human Agility.

'So, then. What do you say to elephants, dear Sharikov?' Philipp Philippovich asked Sharikov mistrustfully.

The latter took offence.

'What, as if I don't understand, or something. A cat's a different matter. Elephants are useful animals,' replied Sharikov.

'Well then, excellent. Since they're useful, go along and look at them. You must obey Ivan Arnoldovich. And no getting into any conversations in the buffet! Ivan Arnoldovich, I most humbly request you not to offer Sharikov any beer.'

Ten minutes later, Ivan Arnoldovich and Sharikov, who was dressed in a cap with a long peak and a thick woollen coat with the collar up, left for the circus. The apartment fell quiet. Philipp Philippovich was in his study. He lit the lamp under its heavy green shade, which made the huge study become very peaceful, and began pacing the room. Long and hot shone the end of his cigar with a pale green light. The professor put his hands in his trouser pockets, and a grave thought troubled his learned brow with its sparse strands of hair. He smacked his lips, sang 'to the sacred banks of the Nile' through his teeth and kept muttering something. Finally he put the cigar aside into the ashtray, went up to a cabinet consisting entirely of glass, and lit the whole study with three extremely powerful lamps from the ceiling. Out of the cabinet, from the third glass shelf, Philipp Philippovich took a narrow jar and, with furrowed brows, began examining it in the light of the lamps. In the transparent and heavy liquid there floated, without falling to the bottom, a small white ball, extracted from the depths of Sharik's brain. Shrugging his shoulders, twisting his lips and snorting, Philipp Philippovich devoured it with his eyes, as though he were trying to discern in the white, buoyant ball the reason for the surprising events that had turned life upside down in the Prechistenka apartment.

It is highly likely that this extremely learned man did discern it. At least, having gazed long enough at the pituitary gland, he put the jar away in the cabinet, locked it, put the key in his waistcoat pocket, and himself collapsed onto the leather of the sofa, pressing his head down into his shoulders and pushing his hands very deep into his jacket pockets. He spent a long time burning a second cigar, completely chewing up its end, and finally, in total solitude, tinted green like a grey-haired Faust, he exclaimed:

'Honest to God, I think I'll risk it.'

Nobody made him any reply to this. In the apartment all sounds had ceased. At eleven o'clock in Obukhov Lane, as is well known, traffic quietens down. Ever so rarely did the distant footsteps of a belated pedestrian ring out, they tapped a while somewhere beyond the curtains and died away. In the study the repeater in his pocket rang gently under Philipp Philippovich's fingers... The professor was waiting impatiently for Dr Bormental and Sharikov to return from the circus.

8

It is not known what it was Philipp Philippovich decided to risk. He did not undertake anything special in the course of the following week and, perhaps in consequence of his inactivity, life in the apartment was filled with events.

Some six days after the incident with the water and the cat, the young man who had turned out to be a woman came from the House Committee to see Sharikov and handed him some documents which Sharikov immediately put in his pocket, and then immediately afterwards he called Dr Bormental.

'Bormental!'

'No, just you call me by my name and patronymic, please!' responded Bormental, changing countenance.

It should be noted that during these six days the surgeon had contrived to fall out with his pupil some eight times. And the atmosphere in the rooms on Obukhov Lane was stifling.

'Well, you call me by my name and patronymic too!' replied Sharikov quite reasonably.

'No!' thundered Philipp Philippovich in the doorway, 'I won't allow you to be called by such a name and patronymic in my apartment. If it's your wish that you should cease to be addressed as "Sharikov" in familiar fashion, both Dr Bormental and I will call you "Master Sharikov".'

'I'm not a master, the masters are all in Paris!' Sharikov barked out.

'Shvonder's work!' cried Philipp Philippovich. 'Well, all right, I'll settle accounts with that wretch. There'll be no one but masters in my apartment as long as I'm in it. Otherwise either you or I will have to leave, most likely you. I shall place an advertisement in the newspapers today and, believe me, I'll find you a room.'

'Oh yeah, I'm such an idiot that I'd go away from here,' replied Sharikov very distinctly.

'What?' asked Philipp Philippovich, and changed countenance to such an extent that Bormental rushed up to him and took him gently and anxiously by the sleeve.

'You know what, don't you be so insolent, *monsieur* Sharikov!' Bormental raised his voice greatly. Sharikov stepped back and pulled out of his pocket three documents – a green, a yellow and a white one – and, jabbing his fingers at them, he began:

'Here. I'm a member of the Housing Association, and I'm due specifically in apartment No. 5 from the responsible tenant, Preobrazhensky, an area of eight square metres.' Sharikov had a think and added a phrase that Bormental noted mechanically in his brain as a new one: 'Be so kind.'

Philipp Philippovich bit his lip, and through it uttered incautiously:

'I swear I'll shoot that Shvonder eventually.'

Sharikov received these words with the highest degree of attention and acuity, as was clear from his eyes.

'Philipp Philippovich, *vorsichtig*[39]...' began Bormental in warning.

'Well, you know what... If something so vile!...' exclaimed Philipp Philippovich in Russian. 'Bear in mind, Sharikov... Master, that if you permit yourself one more insolent outburst, I shall deprive you of dinner and of nourishment in general in my home. Eight metres – that's delightful, but I'm not obliged to feed you on the basis of that frog-coloured paper, am I?'

Here Sharikov took fright and opened his mouth a little.

'I can't remain without sustenance,' he mumbled. 'Where ever will I get my grub?'

'Then behave yourself properly!' declared the two Aesculapiuses in one voice.

Sharikov quietened down significantly and did not do anyone any harm that day with the exception of himself: exploiting Bormental's brief absence, he took possession of his razor and cut his cheekbone open so badly that Philipp Philippovich and Dr Bormental put stitches in the cut, as a result of which Sharikov howled for a long time in floods of tears.

The following night two people sat in the green semi-darkness in the professor's study – Philipp Philippovich himself and the faithful Bormental, who was so attached to him. The house was already asleep. Philipp Philippovich wore his azure dressing gown and red slippers, while Bormental wore a shirt and blue braces. Between the doctors, next to a plump album on the round table, stood a bottle of cognac, a saucer with some pieces of lemon and a cigar box. The scientists, having filled the whole room with smoke, were heatedly discussing the latest event: that evening Sharikov had appropriated two ten-rouble notes that had been lying under a paperweight in Philipp Philippovich's study, had vanished from the apartment and returned late and completely drunk. That was not all. With him had appeared two unknown persons who had made a noise on the main staircase and expressed a desire to stay the night as Sharikov's guests. The aforesaid persons had left only after Fyodor, who had been present during this scene wearing his autumn coat thrown on over the top of his underwear, had telephoned police station No. 45. The persons departed the very instant that Fyodor hung up the receiver. After the persons had gone, it was unclear where the malachite ashtray from the looking glass table in the entrance hall had got to, as well as Philipp Philippovich's beaver hat and his walking stick, on which walking stick was written in gold ornamental script: 'To dear and respected Philipp Philippovich from his grateful house surgeons on the day...' and later came the Roman numeral XXV.

'Who are they?' Philipp Philippovich had advanced, clenching his fists, on Sharikov.

The latter, swaying and sticking to the fur coats, had mumbled to the effect that the persons were unknown to him, that they weren't just some sons of bitches, but nice.

'Most astonishing of all is that they were both drunk, weren't they... How on earth did they manage it?' Philipp Philippovich had marvelled, gazing at the place in the stand where the memento of the anniversary had once been housed.

'Experts,' Fyodor had elucidated, going off to bed with a rouble in his pocket.

Sharikov had categorically denied all knowledge of the two ten-rouble notes, and in so doing had articulated something unclear to the effect that, well, he wasn't the only one in the apartment.

'Aha, perhaps it was Dr Bormental who pinched the banknotes?' Philipp Philippovich had enquired in a voice that was quiet, but strange in tone.

Sharikov had staggered, opened his perfectly drowsy eyes and come out with a suggestion:

'Or perhaps Zinka took them...'

'What's that?' Zina had shouted, appearing in the doorway like a ghost, with the palm of her hand covering the blouse unbuttoned at her breast, 'how does he...'

Philipp Philippovich's neck had flushed a deep red.

'Keep calm, Zinusha,' he had said, reaching out a hand to her, 'don't worry, we'll sort all this out.'

Zina, loose-lipped, had immediately begun wailing, and her palm had started to jump on her collarbone.

'Zina, you should be ashamed of yourself. Who could possibly think it? Ugh, what a disgrace!' Bormental had begun in dismay.

'Well, Zina, you're an idiot, God forgive me,' Philipp Philippovich had tried to say.

But at that point Zina's crying had ceased of its own accord, and everyone had fallen silent. Sharikov had become unwell. Banging his head against the wall, he had emitted a sound – whether 'ee' or 'ye' – something like 'eh-eh-eh!' His face had turned pale and his jaw begun to jerk spasmodically.

'Give him the bucket from the consulting room, the wretch!'

And everyone had started running about, looking after the sick Sharikov. While being led off to bed, swaying in Bormental's arms, he had been swearing very tenderly and melodically, using foul words and pronouncing them with difficulty.

This entire incident had taken place at around one o'clock, and now it was about three in the morning, but the two men in the study were wide awake, wound up by the cognac and lemon. They had smoked so much that the smoke moved in thick, slow strata without even undulating.

Dr Bormental, pale, with very decisive eyes, raised his wasp-waisted glass.

'Philipp Philippovich,' he exclaimed with feeling, 'I shall never forget how I came to you as a half-starved student and you gave me refuge in the Department. Believe me, Philipp Philippovich, you are much more to me than my professor, my teacher... My immeasurable respect for you... Allow me to kiss you, dear Philipp Philippovich.'

'Yes, my dear friend...' Philipp Philippovich murmured in embarrassment and rose to meet him. Bormental embraced him and kissed his fluffy, heavily smoke-laden whiskers.

'Honest to God, Philipp Phili...'

'I'm so moved, so moved... Thank you,' said Philipp Philippovich, 'I sometimes yell at you, my dear friend, during operations. Do forgive an old man's irascibility. Essentially, you know, I'm so lonely... "From Seville unto Granada..."'

'Philipp Philippovich, aren't you ashamed of yourself?...' the ardent Bormental exclaimed sincerely, 'if you don't want to offend me, don't speak to me in such a way again…'

'Well, thank you… "To the sacred banks of the Nile…" Thank you… And I've come to love you as an able doctor.'

'Philipp Philippovich, I'm telling you!' Bormental exclaimed passionately, then darted away, pushed the door leading into the corridor more firmly closed and, returning, continued in a whisper: 'it's the only outcome, you know. Of course, I don't dare to give you advice, but, Philipp Philippovich, take a look at yourself, you're completely worn out, and you simply can't work like this any more!'

'It's absolutely impossible,' Philipp Philippovich confirmed with a sigh.

'Well, then, it's quite unthinkable,' whispered Bormental, 'last time you said you were afraid for me, and if you only knew, dear Professor, how touched I was by that. But after all, I'm not a little boy and I understand for myself what a dreadful thing this could turn out to be. But it's my deep conviction that there's no other way out.'

Philipp Philippovich stood up, waved his arms at him and exclaimed:

'Don't tempt me, don't even say it,' the professor began walking around the room and set waves of smoke a-rocking. 'I won't hear of it. You realise what will happen if we're caught. After all, you and I won't be able to get off on the grounds of "taking background into account", irrespective of it being our first conviction. You haven't got a suitable background, my dear chap, have you?'

'The devil I have! My father was a coroner in Vilno,' replied Bormental mournfully, finishing his cognac.

'Well, there you are, if you like. I mean, that's bad heredity. Nothing nastier could even be imagined. But then I'm afraid mine is even worse. My father was a cathedral archpriest.

Merci. "From Seville unto Granada… In the soft dusk of the nights…" There, damn it.'

'Philipp Philippovich, you're a great figure of global significance, and because of some – excuse the expression – son of a bitch… Pardon me, but can they really touch you?'

'All the more reason for my not entering into this,' Philipp Philippovich retorted pensively, stopping and looking round at the glass cabinet.

'But why?'

'Because, you, after all, are not a great figure of global significance.'

'Of course I'm not…'

'Right then. And abandoning a colleague in the event of a catastrophe, and getting off oneself on the grounds of global significance, forgive me… I'm not Sharikov, I'm a Muscovite student.'

Philipp Philippovich lifted his shoulders proudly and started looking like an ancient French king.

'Philipp Philippovich, oh…' Bormental exclaimed mournfully, 'so, what then? Are you going to wait now until you succeed in making a man out of this hooligan?'

Philipp Philippovich stopped him with a gesture of his hand, poured himself some cognac, knocked it back, sucked on a piece of lemon and began:

'Ivan Arnoldovich, what do you think, do I understand anything about the anatomy and physiology of, well, let's say the human brain mechanism? What's your opinion?'

'Philipp Philippovich, what are you asking?' Bormental replied with great feeling and spread his hands wide.

'Well, all right. No false modesty. I too suppose that in this respect I'm not the last person in Moscow.'

'And I suppose that you are the first, not only in Moscow, but in both London and Oxford too!' Bormental interrupted fiercely.

'Well, fine, so be it. So, then, future Professor Bormental: no one will succeed in that. It's over. You needn't even ask. Just quote me, say: "Preobrazhensky said so". *Finita*[40]. Klim!' Philipp Philippovich suddenly exclaimed triumphantly, and the cabinet answered him with a ringing sound. 'Klim,' he repeated. 'It's like this, Bormental, you're the first pupil of my school and, besides that, you're my friend, as I've become convinced today. So it's you, as a friend, that I'll tell in confidence – of course, I know you won't think of putting me to shame – that old ass Preobrazhensky stumbled through this operation like a third-year student. True, a discovery was made, you know for yourself what it was,' here Philipp Philippovich pointed sadly with both hands at the curtain over the window, evidently alluding to Moscow, 'only bear in mind, Ivan Arnoldovich, that the sole result of that discovery will be that we're all now going to have this Sharikov right here,' Preobrazhensky slapped himself on the neck, steeply sloping and inclined to paralysis, 'rest assured! If somebody,' Philipp Philippovich continued sensuously, 'spread me out here and whipped me, I swear I'd pay some fifty roubles! "From Seville unto Granada…" The devil take me… I mean, I spent five years sitting picking pituitary glands out of brains… Do you know the work I did – it passes understanding. And now one wonders – why? In order one fine day to turn the sweetest dog into such filth that it makes your hair stand on end.'

'Something extraordinary.'

'I agree with you completely. This, Doctor, is the result when a researcher, instead of moving in parallel and in touch with nature, forces a question and lifts a curtain: there, have Sharikov, and like him or lump him.'

'Philipp Philippovich, but what if it were Spinoza's[41] brain?'

'Yes!' roared Philipp Philippovich. 'Yes! If only the ill-fated dog doesn't die on me under the knife. And we've seen the sort of operation it is. In short, I, Philipp Preobrazhensky, never did anything more difficult in my life. One can implant the pituitary gland from Spinoza or any other devil of the sort and create a being of extremely high standing from a dog. But why bother, one wonders. Explain to me, please, why one needs to fabricate Spinozas artificially, when a woman can give birth to him any time you like. After all, Madame Lomonosova gave birth in Kholmogory to that famous son of hers.[42] Doctor, mankind takes care of it itself, and every year in evolutionary order, singling them out from the mass of various sorts of filth, it persistently creates dozens of outstanding geniuses who adorn the earth. Now you can see, Doctor, why I discredited your conclusion in Sharikov's case history. My discovery, may the devil take it, which you're making such a fuss over, is worth precisely one bent groat... Don't argue, Ivan Arnoldovich, it's so, I understand it now, you see. And I never engage in idle talk, as you know very well. Yes, all right, in theory, it's interesting! The physiologists will be in raptures. Moscow's raving... Well, but in practice, what of it? Who is before you now?' Preobrazhensky pointed his finger in the direction of the consulting room where Sharikov was slumbering.

'An extraordinary scoundrel.'

'But who is he? Klim, Klim,' cried the professor, 'Klim Chugunkin,' (Bormental opened his mouth) 'this is what, sir: two convictions, alcoholism, "share everything out", a hat and twenty roubles gone,' (here Philipp Philippovich remembered the anniversary stick and turned crimson) 'a lout and a swine... Well, I'll find that stick. In short, the pituitary gland is a closed chamber defining a man's given identity. Given! "From Seville unto Granada..."' shouted Philipp Philippovich, rolling his eyes wildly, 'but not mankind's in general. It is, in miniature, the brain itself. And I have absolutely no need of it, may it go to the devil. I was concerned with something else entirely, with eugenics, with the improvement of the human species. And then I stumbled upon rejuvenation. Do you really think I perform them for the money? I am a scientist, after all.'

'You're a great scientist, that's what!' said Bormental, gulping cognac. His eyes were bloodshot.

'I wanted to do a little experiment after I first got an extract of sex hormone from the pituitary gland two years ago. And what was the result instead of that? O my God! Those hormones in the pituitary gland, O Lord... Doctor, before me is dim hopelessness, I swear, I've lost my way.'

Bormental suddenly rolled up his sleeves and pronounced, slanting his eyes towards his nose:

'Then the thing is, dear teacher, if you don't want to, at my own risk I'll feed him arsenic myself. To hell with my father being a coroner. I mean, in the end he's your own experimental creature.'

Philipp Philippovich's fire went out, he went soft, collapsed into an armchair and said:

'No, I won't allow you to do it, my dear boy. I'm sixty years old, I can give you advice. Never enter into a crime, no matter who it might be directed against. Live through into old age with your hands clean.'

'For pity's sake, Philipp Philippovich, if that Shvonder works on him some more, whatever will become of him?! My God, I'm only now beginning to realise what might result from this Sharikov!'

'Aha! You realise now? Well I realised ten days after the operation. And the thing is, it's Shvonder that's the biggest fool. He doesn't realise that Sharikov is a more threatening danger for him than for me. Well, at the moment he's trying to set him on me in various ways, without grasping that if somebody in turn sets Sharikov on Shvonder, nothing will be left of him but his horns and hoofs.'

'I'll say! You only have to look at the cats! A man with a dog's heart.'

'Oh no, no,' replied Philipp Philippovich in a drawl, 'you're making the gravest error, Doctor, for God's sake, don't slander the dog. The cats – that's a temporary thing... That's a question of discipline and two or three weeks. I assure you. Another month or so, and he'll stop attacking them.'

'And why not now?'

'Ivan Arnoldovich, it's elementary... Really, what are you asking? The pituitary gland won't just hang in mid-air, will it? I mean, it is after all attached to a dog's brain, so give it a chance to settle in. Sharikov is already now displaying only the vestiges of what is canine, and you must understand that the cats are the best thing of all that he does. Consider that the whole horror lies in the fact that he already has not a dog's, but a human heart. And the lousiest of all there are in nature!'

Bormental, wound up to the highest degree, clenched his strong, thin hands into fists, flexed his shoulders and said firmly:

'Enough. I'll kill him!'

'I forbid it!' replied Philipp Philippovich categorically.

'But for Heaven's sake...'

Philipp Philippovich suddenly pricked up his ears, raised a finger.

'Wait a minute... I heard footsteps.'

They both listened carefully, but it was quiet in the corridor.

'I imagined it,' said Philipp Philippovich and began to speak heatedly in German. The Russian word 'felony' was heard several times in his words.

'One moment,' Bormental suddenly pricked up his ears and strode to the door. Footsteps were clearly audible and were close to the study. In addition a voice was burbling. Bormental flung the doors open and recoiled in astonishment. An utterly stunned Philipp Philippovich froze in the armchair.

In the illuminated rectangle of the corridor appeared Darya Petrovna wearing only her nightshirt and with a belligerent and blazing face. Both the doctor and the professor were dazzled by the abundance of powerful and, as it seemed to both of them in their terror, completely bare flesh. In her mighty hands Darya Petrovna was dragging something, and that 'something' was digging its heels in, sitting on its backside, and its little legs, covered in black down, were stumbling over the parquet. The 'something' proved, of course, to be Sharikov, completely lost, still tipsy, all tousled and wearing only his shirt.

Darya Petrovna, vast and naked, shook Sharikov like a sack of potatoes and pronounced the following words:

'Feast your eyes, Mr Professor, on our visitor, Telegraph Telegraphovich. I've been married, but Zina's an innocent young girl. It's a good thing I woke up.'

Having finished this speech, Darya Petrovna plunged into a state of shame, shrieked, covered her breast with her arms and rushed off.

'Darya Petrovna, for God's sake excuse me,' a red Philipp Philippovich, coming to his senses, cried after her.

Bormental rolled the sleeves of his shirt up a little higher and moved towards Sharikov. Philipp Philippovich glanced into his eyes and was horrified.

'Doctor, what are you doing! I forbid…'

With his right hand Bormental took Sharikov by the scruff of the neck and shook him so hard that the linen at the back of his shirt split, and a button flew off from the collar at the front.

Philipp Philippovich rushed to get between them and started tearing puny Sharikov out of the tenacious surgical hands.

'You've no right to go mixing it!' shouted the half-strangled Sharikov, sitting down on the floor and sobering up.

'Doctor!' wailed Philipp Philippovich.

Bormental recovered himself somewhat and let Sharikov go, after which the latter immediately began snivelling.

'Well, all right,' hissed Bormental, 'we'll wait until morning. I'll give him a dressing down when he's sober.'

Here he took Sharikov by the armpits and dragged him into the waiting room to sleep.

At this Sharikov made an attempt to kick out, but his legs would not obey.

Philipp Philippovich set his legs apart, as a result of which his azure skirts parted, he raised his arms and eyes to the ceiling light in the corridor and said:

'Well I never...'

9

Sharikov's dressing down, as promised by Dr Bormental, did not take place the following morning, however, for the reason that Polygraph Polygraphovich had disappeared from home. Bormental fell into furious despair, cursing himself as an ass for failing to hide the key to the front door, shouted that it was unforgivable, and ended with the wish that Sharikov should fall under a bus. Philipp Philippovich sat in the study with his fingers thrust into his hair and said:

'I can imagine what will happen out in the street... I can ima-a-gine. "From Seville unto Granada". My God.'

'He may yet be in the House Committee,' raged Bormental, and went running off somewhere.

In the House Committee he had such a row with Chairman Shvonder that the latter sat down to write a statement to send to the People's Court of the Khamovniki District, shouting as he did so that he was not a watchman for Professor Preobrazhensky's charge, particularly as that charge, Polygraph, had proved as recently as the day before to be a scoundrel, having taken seven roubles from the House Committee, allegedly for the purchase of textbooks from a cooperative.

Fyodor, who earned three roubles for the job, searched the whole building from top to bottom. Nowhere were any traces of Sharikov to be found.

Only one thing became clear – that Polygraph had departed at dawn, wearing cap, scarf and overcoat, taking with him a bottle of rowan-berry liqueur from the sideboard, Dr Bormental's gloves, and all of his own documents. Darya Petrovna and Zina concealed nothing, and expressed their boisterous delight and their hope that Sharikov would return no more. The day before, Sharikov had borrowed three roubles fifty kopeks from Darya Petrovna.

'Serves you right!' growled Philipp Philippovich, shaking his fists. All day long the telephone rang, and the telephone rang on the next day. The doctors saw an unusual number of patients, but in the study on the third day the question arose in earnest about the need to inform the police, who would have to seek Sharikov out in the murky depths of Moscow.

And no sooner had the word 'police' been pronounced than the reverential quiet of Obukhov Lane was cut by the bark of a lorry, and the windows in the building shook. Then a confident ring was heard, and Polygraph Polygraphovich appeared in the entrance hall. Both the professor and the doctor went out to meet him. Polygraph entered with exceptional dignity, in complete silence he took off his cap, his overcoat he hung on the antlers, and he appeared in a new guise. He was wearing a second-hand leather jacket, worn trousers, also leather, and English high boots with lacing up to the knees. An unbelievable smell of tomcats immediately spread through the entire entrance hall. As if by order Preobrazhensky and Bormental folded their arms on their chests, stood by the door frame and awaited Polygraph Polygraphovich's first announcements. He smoothed down his coarse hair, coughed and looked around in such a way that it was clear: Polygraph wanted to conceal his embarrassment with the aid of nonchalance.

'Philipp Philippovich,' he finally began saying, 'I have taken up an appointment.'

Both doctors emitted an indefinite dry sound from their throats and stirred. Preobrazhensky came to his senses first, reached out his hand and said:

'Give me the document.'

It was typed: 'The bearer hereof, Comrade Polygraph Polygraphovich Sharikov, is confirmed to be Head of the Sub-division for the Cleansing of the City of Moscow of Stray Animals (Cats etc.) in a department of the M.C.A.[43]'

'So,' said Philipp Philippovich heavily, 'who was it that fixed you up? Ah, I can guess for myself anyway.'

'Well, yes, Shvonder,' replied Sharikov.

'Permit me to ask you why you smell so disgusting?'

Sharikov sniffed the jacket anxiously.

'Well, so, there's a smell... of course: it goes with the work. Yesterday we were strangling cats one after another...'

Philipp Philippovich winced and looked at Bormental. The latter's eyes were reminiscent of two black gun muzzles aimed point-blank at Sharikov. Without any sort of foreword he moved towards Sharikov and took him easily and confidently by the gullet.

'Help!' squeaked Sharikov, turning pale.

'Doctor!'

'I won't allow myself to do anything bad, Philipp Philippovich, don't worry,' Bormental responded in a voice of iron, and called out: 'Zina and Darya Petrovna!'

They appeared in the entrance hall.

'Right, repeat after me,' said Bormental, and squeezed Sharikov's throat a little closer towards a fur coat, 'I'm sorry...'

'Well, all right, I'm repeating,' replied the utterly stunned Sharikov in a croaky voice. He suddenly took in some air, gave a jerk and tried to cry 'help', but the cry did not emerge, and his head was completely buried in the fur coat.

'Doctor, I implore you.'

Sharikov began nodding his head, indicating that he submitted and would repeat after him.

'...I'm sorry, much respected Darya Petrovna and Zinaida?...'

'Prokofyevna,' whispered Zina in fright.

'Phew. Prokofyevna...' said the hoarse Sharikov, gulping in air, '...that I allowed myself...'

'Myself a vile prank in the night in a state of intoxication.'

'Intoxication.'

'Never again will I...'

'Will I...'

'Let him go, let him go, Ivan Arnoldovich,' begged both women simultaneously, 'you'll strangle him.'

Bormental let Sharikov go free and said:

'Is the lorry waiting for you?'

'No,' replied Polygraph respectfully, 'it only brought me here.'

'Zina, let the vehicle go. Now bear in mind the following: have you returned once more to Philipp Philippovich's apartment?'

'Where else am I to go?' replied Sharikov timidly with his eyes roaming around.

'Excellent. You're to be as quiet as a mouse. Otherwise for every outrageous prank you'll have to have dealings with me. Understood?'

'Understood,' replied Sharikov.

Philipp Philippovich maintained silence all the time violence was being used against Sharikov. Pitiful somehow, he shrank by the door frame and bit a fingernail with his eyes lowered to the parquet. Then he suddenly raised them to Sharikov and asked, indistinctly and mechanically:

'And what do you do with those... with the cats that are killed?'

'They'll go to make coats,' replied Sharikov, 'they'll turn them into squirrels to sell to workers on credit.'

Hereupon a silence came over the apartment and lasted for two days.

Polygraph Polygraphovich would leave in the morning in a lorry, appear in the evening and have dinner quietly in the company of Philipp Philippovich and Bormental.

Despite the fact that Bormental and Sharikov slept in the

same room, the waiting room, they did not converse with one another, so Bormental was the first to get bored.

A couple of days later, a slim young woman wearing eye make-up and cream-coloured stockings appeared in the apartment and became very confused at the sight of the apartment's magnificence. In a threadbare little coat she followed after Sharikov, and in the entrance hall bumped into the professor.

The latter, dumbfounded, stopped, narrowed his eyes and asked:

'Permit me to learn?'

'I'm getting married to her, this is our typist, she's going to live with me. Bormental will have to be moved out of the waiting room. He's got his own apartment,' Sharikov elucidated, extremely antagonistic and sullen.

Philipp Philippovich blinked his eyes a little, had a think, gazing at the young woman who had turned crimson, and very politely gave her an invitation.

'Can I ask you to come into my study for a moment?'

'And I'll come with her,' said Sharikov quickly and suspiciously.

And at this point Bormental instantly materialised as if from out of the ground.

'I'm sorry,' he said, 'the professor will have a chat with the lady, while you and I will spend some time here.'

'I don't want to,' responded Sharikov bad-temperedly, trying to head after the young woman, who was burning with fear, and Philipp Philippovich.

'No, forgive me,' Bormental took Sharikov by the wrist and they went into the consulting room.

For five minutes or so nothing was heard from the study, but then suddenly the young woman's muffled sobbing could be made out.

Philipp Philippovich was standing by the desk, while the young woman cried into a dirty lace handkerchief.

'The wretch, he said he was wounded in battle,' the young woman sobbed.

'He's lying,' replied Philipp Philippovich adamantly. He shook his head and continued. 'I'm sincerely sorry for you, but you simply can't do this with the first man you meet just because of his official position... I mean, it's outrageous, child... Here now...' He opened a drawer in his desk and took out three thirty-rouble notes.

'I'll poison myself,' the young woman wept, 'it's salted meat in the canteen every day... and he's threatening... says he's a Red Army commander... with me, he says, you'll live in a luxury apartment... pineapples every day... I've got a kind, he says, personality, I only hate cats... He took my ring as a keepsake...'

'Come, come, come, a kind personality... "From Seville unto Granada,"' muttered Philipp Philippovich, 'you have to get over it – you're still so young...'

'Surely not in that gateway there?'

'Come, take the money while it's being offered, as a loan,' rasped Philipp Philippovich.

Then the doors flew open ceremoniously, and Bormental, at Philipp Philippovich's invitation, led in Sharikov. The latter's eyes were darting to and fro, and the coat on his head stood up like a brush.

'Bastard,' the young woman pronounced, flashing her tear-stained, smudged eyes and her striped, powdered nose.

'Why do you have a scar on your forehead? Be so good as to explain to this lady,' asked Philipp Philippovich insinuatingly.

Sharikov staked everything:

'I was wounded on the Kolchak fronts,'[44] he barked.

The young woman stood up and went out, crying loudly.

'Stop it!' Philipp Philippovich cried after her, 'wait, the ring, if you please,' he said, turning to Sharikov.

The latter submissively removed a hollow emerald ring from his finger.

'Well, all right,' he suddenly said maliciously, 'I'll make sure you remember this. I'll be arranging a staff reduction for you tomorrow.'

'Don't be afraid of him,' Bormental cried after her, 'I won't let him do anything.' He turned and looked at Sharikov in such a way that the latter retreated and hit the back of his head on a cabinet.

'What's her surname?' Bormental asked him. 'Her surname!' he roared, and suddenly became wild and terrifying.

'Vasnetsova,' replied Sharikov, looking to see how he could slip away.

'On a daily basis,' uttered Bormental, taking hold of the lapel of Sharikov's jacket, 'I shall personally enquire in the Cleansing Department whether Citizen Vasnetsova has been dismissed. And if you so much as… if I find out that she has… I shall personally shoot you down on this very spot. Beware, Sharikov – I'm telling you in plain Russian!'

Sharikov stared fixedly at Bormental's nose.

'We'll find revolvers ourselves,' mumbled Polygraph, but very limply, and he suddenly managed to spurt out of the room.

'Beware!' Bormental's cry carried after him.

For the night and for half of the following day the quiet hung like a cloud before a storm. Everyone was silent. But the following day, when Polygraph Polygraphovich, who had been pricked in the morning by a nasty foreboding, left gloomy in the lorry for his place of work, Professor Preobrazhensky saw one of his former patients at a quite untimely hour, a fat and strapping man in military uniform. The latter had been persistent in seeking a meeting and had got it. On entering the study he politely clicked his heels towards the professor.

'Have your pains resumed, my dear fellow?' asked a pinched-looking Philipp Philippovich, 'please take a seat.'

'*Merci*. No, Professor,' replied the guest, standing his helmet on the corner of the desk, 'I'm very grateful to you... Hm... I've come to see you on a different matter, Philipp Philippovich... having great respect... hm... to warn you. Obviously rubbish. Simply he's a scoundrel...' The patient reached into his briefcase and took out a piece of paper, 'it's a good thing it was reported directly to me...'

Philipp Philippovich saddled his nose with a pince-nez on top of his spectacles and began to read. He muttered to himself for a long time, changing in countenance with every line. '...and also threatening to kill the Chairman of the House Committee, Comrade Shvonder, from which it is clear he keeps firearms. And he makes counter-revolutionary speeches and even ordered his social-womanservant Zinaida Prokofyevna Bunina to burn Engels in the stove, like a blatant Menshevik with his assistant Bormental, Ivan Arnoldovich, who is secretly resident in his apartment without being registered. Signature of the Head of the Subdivision for Cleansing, P.P. Sharikov, certified by Chairman of the House Committee, Shvonder, and Secretary, Pestrukhin.'

'Will you allow me to keep this?' asked Philipp Philippovich with blotches appearing all over him, 'or, I'm sorry, perhaps you need it to let the matter take its proper legal course?'

'Forgive me, Professor,' said the patient, greatly offended, and flared his nostrils, 'you really do regard us very disdainfully. I...' – and here he began puffing himself up like a turkeycock.

'No, forgive me, forgive me, my dear fellow!' Philipp Philippovich mumbled, 'I'm sorry, truly, I didn't mean to offend you.'

'We know how to read documents, Philipp Philippovich!'

'Don't be angry, my dear fellow, he's worn me out to such a degree...'

'So I imagine,' the patient calmed down fully, 'but what scum, all the same! It'd be interesting to take a glance at him. There are some real legends being told about you in Moscow...'

Philipp Philippovich only waved his hand despairingly. At this point the patient discerned that the professor had become hunched and even seemed to have gone grey of late.

* * *

The crime ripened, and fell like a stone, as is indeed usually the way. With a gnawing and troubled heart Polygraph Polygraphovich returned in the lorry. Philipp Philippovich's voice invited him into the consulting room. The surprised Sharikov came and with vague terror glanced into the gun muzzles in Bormental's face and then at Philipp Philippovich. A dark cloud was floating around the assistant, and his left hand, holding a cigarette, was quivering slightly on the shiny handle of the obstetric chair.

With very ominous composure Philipp Philippovich said:

'Now collect your things: your trousers, overcoat, everything you need – and get out of the apartment!'

'What do you mean?' said Sharikov in sincere surprise.

'Get out of the apartment – today,' repeated Philipp Philippovich in a monotone, squinting at his nails.

Some evil spirit had evidently taken up residence in Polygraph Polygraphovich, death already lay in wait for him and fate stood at his shoulder. He himself rushed into the embrace of the inevitable and woofed out bad-temperedly and abruptly:

'Now what is all this at the end of the day! What, won't I be able to find a law against you, or something? I'm sitting on my eight metres here and I'm staying.'

'Clear out of the apartment,' whispered Philipp Philippovich earnestly.

Sharikov invited his death himself. He raised his left hand and with bitten fingernails and an intolerable smell of cats gave Philipp Philippovich a V-sign. And then with his right hand, aiming at the dangerous Bormental, he drew from his pocket a revolver. Bormental's cigarette fell like a falling star, and a few seconds later Philipp Philippovich, jumping over broken glass, was rushing in horror from cabinet to couch. Upon it, outstretched and wheezing, lay the Head of the Subdivision for Cleansing, and on his chest was the surgeon Bormental, suffocating him with a small white pillow.

A few minutes later Dr Bormental, not looking himself, went through to the front entrance and stuck up a note next to the bell-push:

'No surgery today on account of Professor's illness. Please do not disturb by ringing.'

With a shiny penknife he cut the wire of the bell, in the mirror he examined his badly scratched and bloody face and his lacerated hands that jumped with little tremors. Then he appeared in the kitchen doorway and said to the wary Zina and Darya Petrovna:

'The professor requests you not to leave the apartment.'

'Very well,' replied Zina and Darya Petrovna timidly.

'Allow me to lock the door to the rear entrance and take the key away,' began Bormental, hiding in the shadow behind the door and covering his face with his palm. 'It's temporary, not because you're not trusted. But if someone comes, you'll give in and open up, and we mustn't be disturbed. We're busy.'

'Very well,' the women replied, and at once became pale.

Bormental locked the rear entrance, took the key away,

locked the main entrance, locked the door from the corridor into the entrance hall, and his footsteps died away by the consulting room.

Silence covered the apartment, crawled into every corner. Dusk came on, nasty, wary, in a word, gloom. True, neighbours across the courtyard said subsequently that all Professor Preobrazhensky's lights in the consulting room windows that looked out into the courtyard had apparently been burning that evening, and even that they had apparently seen the white cap of the professor himself. It is difficult to check. True, when it was already over, Zina chattered too about how, after Bormental and the professor had left the consulting room, Ivan Arnoldovich had frightened her to death in the study by the fireplace. He had allegedly been squatting in the study and personally burning in the fireplace a notebook in a blue binding from the batch in which the case histories of the professor's patients were written down. The doctor's face was apparently quite green, and all, well, all... scratched to pieces. And Philipp Philippovich did not look himself that evening. And also that... but still, perhaps the innocent girl from the Prechistenka apartment is lying...

One thing can be vouched for: in the apartment on that evening there was the most complete and awful silence.

Epilogue

Ten days to the night after the battle in the consulting room in Professor Preobrazhensky's apartment on Obukhov Lane, there was an abrupt ring. The voices outside the door frightened Zina to death.

'Criminal police and an investigator. Have the kindness to open up.'

Running footsteps began, knocking began, they started to enter, and in the waiting room, glittering with lights and with newly glazed cabinets, there appeared a mass of people. A couple in policemen's uniform, one in a black overcoat with a briefcase, the pale and gloating Chairman Shvonder, the youth-cum-woman, Fyodor the doorman, Zina, Darya Petrovna and a half-dressed Bormental, bashfully covering up his tieless neck.

The door from the study let Philipp Philippovich through. He emerged in the azure dressing gown well known to everyone, and right there all were able to satisfy themselves immediately that Philipp Philippovich had greatly recovered during the past week. The former masterful and energetic Philipp Philippovich, full of dignity, stood before the nocturnal guests and apologised for being in his dressing gown.

'Don't feel awkward, Professor,' responded the man in civilian dress in great embarrassment, then he started to dither and began: 'It's very unpleasant. We have a warrant for a search of your apartment, and…' the man gave Philipp Philippovich's whiskers a sidelong glance and concluded: 'and for your arrest, depending on the result.'

Philipp Philippovich narrowed his eyes and asked:

'Accused of what, dare I ask, and by whom?'

The man gave his cheek a scratch and began reading out from a document from his briefcase:

' "On the charge made against Preobrazhensky, Bormental, Zinaida Bunina and Darya Ivanova of the murder of the Head of the Subdivision for Cleansing of the M.C.A., Polygraph Polygraphovich Sharikov." '

Zina's sobbing drowned the end of his words. There was commotion.

'I don't understand a thing,' replied Philipp Philippovich, jerking up his shoulders regally, 'what Sharikov is that? Ah, I'm sorry, that dog of mine... on which I operated?'

'Forgive me, Professor, not the dog, but when he was already human. That's the thing.'

'That is, he talked?' asked Philipp Philippovich, 'that doesn't yet mean being human. Still, that's unimportant. Sharik exists even now, and no one has killed him, that's for sure.'

'Professor,' began the black man in great surprise, raising his brows, 'then he must be presented. It's the tenth day since he disappeared, and the information, if you'll excuse me, is very bad.'

'Dr Bormental, have the kindness to present Sharik to the investigator,' ordered Philipp Philippovich, taking possession of the warrant.

Dr Bormental went out with a crooked smile.

When he returned and whistled, out of the study door after him leapt a dog of strange character. It was bald in patches, in patches its coat was growing. It came out, like a trained circus performer, on its hind legs, then dropped onto all four and looked around. A deathly silence congealed in the waiting room like jelly. The nightmarish-looking dog with a crimson scar on its forehead rose onto its hind legs and, with a smile, sat down in an armchair.

The second policeman suddenly crossed himself with sweeping movements and, stepping back, trod on both Zina's feet at once.

The man in black, without closing his mouth, uttered the following:

'But how, if you please? He worked in Cleansing...'

'I didn't appoint him there,' replied Philipp Philippovich. 'Mr Shvonder gave him a recommendation, if I'm not mistaken.'

'I don't understand a thing,' the black man said in bewilderment and turned to the first policeman: 'Is that him?'

'It's him,' replied the police officer soundlessly. 'Positively him.'

'The very man,' Fyodor's voice was heard, 'only he's all hairy again, the scumbag.'

'But he talked... ahem... ahem...'

'And he still talks now, only less and less, so make the most of the opportunity, because he'll soon fall completely silent.'

'But why?' the black man quietly enquired.

Philipp Philippovich shrugged his shoulders.

'Science does not yet know ways of turning animals into men. Now I tried, only unsuccessfully, as you can see. It talked a little and then began to revert to the primitive state. Atavism.'

'Indecent language forbidden!' the dog suddenly barked out from the armchair and got up.

The black man turned pale all of a sudden, dropped his briefcase and started to fall sideways, a police officer caught him from the side, and Fyodor from behind. There was chaos, and in it three phrases were heard most distinctly of all:

Philipp Philippovich's: 'Tincture of valerian. It's a faint.'

Dr Bormental's: 'I shall personally throw Shvonder down the stairs, if he appears in Professor Preobrazhensky's apartment again.'

And Shvonder's: 'Please include those words in the report.'

* * *

The grey concertinas of the pipes warmed. The curtains hid the dense Prechistenka night with its solitary star. The superior being, the grand canine philanthropist sat in an armchair, while Sharik the dog, having settled down, lay on the rug by the leather sofa. In the mornings, because of the March mist, the dog suffered from headaches which tortured him in a ring around the seam on his head. But they went away by the evening thanks to the warmth. And now he was feeling better and better, and the thoughts in the dog's head flowed smooth and warm.

'I've been so lucky, so lucky,' he thought, dozing off, 'simply indescribably lucky. I'm firmly established in this apartment. I'm absolutely certain there's something impure in my background. There's something of the Newfoundland there. She was a trollop, my grandmother, may she rest in peace, the old girl. Firmly established. True, my head's been covered in welts for some reason, but it'll heal up before too long. There's no need to pay any attention to that.'

* * *

In the distance there was a muffled clinking of phials. The bitten one was tidying up in the consulting room cabinets.

But the grey-haired magician was sitting and singing:

' "To the sacred banks of the Nile…" '

The dog saw terrible things. The grand man plunged hands wearing slippery gloves into a vessel, took brains out – the persistent, insistent man was always trying to achieve something, cutting, examining, narrowing his eyes and singing:

' "To the sacred banks of the Nile…" '

– Moscow, January-March 1925

Notes

1. A large area of woodland and park in the north of Moscow.
2. A phrase from Radames' aria from the opera *Aïda* (1870) by Giuseppe Verdi (1813–1901).
3. 'Persian thread' (French).
4. Crayfish Necks are a type of boiled sweet and Abrau Durso a North Caucasian sparkling wine.
5. A central Moscow street known for the sale of hunting equipment and game.
6. The Moscow Association of Industrial Enterprises for Processing Agricultural Produce. There is an allusion here to Vladimir Mayakovsky's advertising slogan for the organisation in use from 1923, 'Nowhere but from / Mosselprom.'
7. The Moscow Union of Consumers' Societies.
8. Sharik's bewilderment would have been accentuated by the shop owners' name echoing the Russian word for 'blueness', *golubizna*, and their shop being located on Butchers' Street (*myasnik* meaning 'butcher').
9. A.V. Chichkin was the owner of a chain of dairies in Moscow.
10. The proprietors of Moscow's best-known grocery store.
11. Here and throughout the story the professor is singing fragments of Don Juan's serenade from the dramatic poem *Don Juan* (1860) by Alexei Konstantinovich Tolstoy (1817–75), set to music by P.I. Tchaikovsky in 1878.
12. 'Word of honour' (French).
13. The Association of Moscow State Factories in the Fat and Bone Processing Industry produced cosmetics.
14. It was customary in Moscow addresses to designate a house by its owner's name rather than by a number.
15. The pro-Bolshevik American dancer (1877–1927) opened a school of dancing on Prechistenka in 1921, but left Russia for good in September 1924.
16. The Assyrian queen of the 9th century BC, credited with the creation of the hanging gardens of Babylon.
17. A new brand of weak vodka had received the blessing of the Chairman of the Soviet of Peoples' Commissars, A.I. Rykov (after whom it was named *rykovka*), and appeared in the shops in 1924.
18. One of Moscow's best-known restaurants.
19. The German philosopher (1818–83) was the inspiration of Lenin and the Bolsheviks.
20. The date coincides with the Bolshevik conference in Petrograd that adopted Lenin's April Theses, his programme for the party's seizure of power.
21. Friedrich Engels (1820–95) was the coauthor, with Marx, of the *Communist Manifesto* (1848); Nikolai Romanov is Tsar Nicholas II (1868–1918).

22. I.I. Mechnikov (1845–1916), a Nobel Prize winner for work on immunology, took an active interest in questions of rejuvenation and extension of the span of human life.

23. Muir and Mirrielees, a department store alongside the Bolshoi Theatre.

24. A song sung by the priests' choir in Verdi's *Aïda* (see note 2).

25. In J.W. von Goethe's *Faust*, a work with themes of rejuvenation that link its hero with Preobrazhensky, a homunculus is created by Faust's assistant, Wagner.

26. D.I. Mendeleyev (1834–1907), creator of the periodic table of elements.

27. Kuznetsky Bridge, one of Moscow's premier shopping streets.

28. This is a pejorative diminutive that contrasts with Preobrazhensky's affectionate 'Zinusha'.

29. A businessman who has profited from the introduction of Lenin's New Economic Policy (N.E.P.) in 1922.

30. The Russian Soviet Federal Socialist Republic.

31. Orthodox Russians christened their children by reference to the church calendar, with children being named after a saint's day close to their birthday. Sharikov has chosen his name from a reference to a printers' holiday in a post-revolutionary calendar.

32. An exemption from military service for medical reasons.

33. In Greek mythology, Aesculapius, the son of Apollo, the god of medicine, was a healer and physician who himself became a demigod.

34. 'Later' (German).

35. 'Very good' (German).

36. The eponymous hero of *The Life and Adventures of Robinson Crusoe* (1720) by Daniel Defoe (1660–1731).

37. K.J. Kautsky (1854–1938) was a leader of the German Social Democrats and the Second International but was antipathetic to Bolshevism.

38. The Yussems were a Spanish family of aerial acrobats on tour in Moscow early in 1925, and The Dead Centre Man was a balancing act.

39. 'Careful' (German).

40. 'It's over' (Italian).

41. Baruch (Benedict) de Spinoza (1632–77), the Dutch philosopher and theologian.

42. Russia's great polymath Mikhail Vasilyevich Lomonosov (1711–65) was born into a humble fisherman's family on the remote White Sea, yet came to be the founder of Moscow University.

43. Moscow Communal Administration.

44. During the Civil War the opposition to the Bolsheviks in Siberia had been led by Admiral A.V. Kolchak (1874–1920) until his capture and execution.

Biographical note

Mikhail Bulgakov was born in Kiev in 1891. In 1909 he entered medical school, where he began writing; his early stories were based on his medical experiences, and resulted in his *Notes of a Young Doctor*. In 1913 he married Tatyana Lappa, and she proved a considerable support when he was later to suffer from a morphine addiction. He worked as a doctor in Kiev in the years 1918 and 1919, where he witnessed first the German occupation, and then the invasion of the Red Army. Soon after this he gave up medicine in favour of pursuing a writing career; he had, by this time, written numerous short stories and a number of plays for local theatres.

In 1921 he moved to Moscow, where he worked for a Berlin journal and for the newspaper *Gudok* [*The Whistle*], among others. His first collection of short stories, *Diaboliad*, was published in 1925; that same year he wrote *A Dog's Heart*, only to see it confiscated by the police. He was by now facing increasing pressure from his communist critics and, in 1928, he was refused permission to travel abroad. It was forbidden for his plays to be performed, although this did not prevent Bulgakov from continuing writing; in 1928 he had begun what was to be his masterpiece, *The Master and Margarita*.

Around this time he began petitioning Stalin for permission to leave Russia. Stalin refused, but allowed Bulgakov's play *The Day of the Turbins* to be staged. The conflict between the artist and the State from then on became the key theme in Bulgakov's writing. He continued working on *The Master and Margarita* until his death in 1940, and although it was published some years after his death, the full, uncensored version did not appear until 1989.

Hugh Aplin studied Russian at the University of East Anglia and Voronezh State University, and worked at the Universities of Leeds and St Andrews before taking up his post as Head of Russian at Westminster School, London. His previous translations include Mikhail Bulgakov's *The Fatal Eggs*, Anton Chekhov's *The Story of a Nobody*, Nikolai Gogol's *The Squabble*, Fyodor Dostoevsky's *Poor People*, Leo Tolstoy's *Hadji Murat* and Ivan Turgenev's *Faust*, all published by Hesperus Press

FULL LIST OF TITLES IN THE HESPERUS 2012 ANNIVERSARY REPRINTS SERIES

Author	Title	Foreword writer
Jane Austen	*Love and Friendship*	Fay Weldon
Mikhail Bulgakov	*A Dog's Heart*	A.S. Byatt
Charlotte Brontë	*The Secret*	Salley Vickers
Wilkie Collins	*The Frozen Deep*	
Joseph Conrad	*Heart of Darkness*	A.N. Wilson
Charles Dickens	*The Haunted House*	Peter Ackroyd
Fyodor Dostoevsky	*Notes from the Underground*	Will Self
Nathaniel Hawthorne	*Rappaccini's Daughter*	Simon Schama
Prosper Mérimée	*Carmen*	Philip Pullman
Mark Twain	*The Diary of Adam and Eve*	John Updike

HESPERUS PRESS BESTSELLERS

Author	Title	Foreword writer
Pietro Aretino	*The Secret Life of Nuns*	
Pietro Aretino	*The Secret Life of Wives*	Paul Bailey
Jane Austen	*Sanditon*	A.C. Grayling
Jane Austen	*The Watsons*	Kate Atkinson
Aphra Behn	*The Lover's Watch*	
Charlotte Brontë	*The Spell*	Nicola Barker
Giacomo Casanova	*The Duel*	Tim Parks
Anton Chekhov	*Three Years*	William Fiennes
Wilkie Collins	*Who Killed Zebedee?*	Martin Jarvis
Arthur Conan Doyle	*The Tragedy of the Korosko*	Tony Robinson
Cyrano de Bergerac	*Journey to the Moon*	Andrew Smith
Daniel Defoe	*The King of Pirates*	Peter Ackroyd
Charles Dickens	*The Holly-Tree Inn*	
Charles Dickens	*Mrs Lirriper*	Philip Hensher
Charles Dickens	*Mugby Junction*	Robert Macfarlane
Charles Dickens	*Somebody's Luggage*	Philippa Stockley
Charles Dickens	*The Wreck of the Golden Mary*	Simon Callow
Elizabeth Gaskell	*The Moorland Cottage*	
Théophile Gautier	*The Jinx*	Gilbert Adair
Johann Wolfgang von Goethe	*The Man of Fifty*	A.S. Byatt
Nikolai Gogol	*The Squabble*	Patrick McCabe
Henry James	*In the Cage*	Libby Purves
Henry James	*The Lesson of the Master*	Colm Tóibín
Franz Kafka	*Metamorphosis*	Martin Jarvis
Franz Kafka	*The Trial*	Zadie Smith
Mikhail Kuzmin	*Wings*	Paul Bailey
D.H. Lawrence	*Daughters of the Vicar*	Anita Desai
Jack London	*The Scarlet Plague*	Tony Robinson

Contemporary & Modern fiction

Author	Title	Foreword writer
Ilya Boyashov	*The Way of Muri*	
Karel Čapek	*Rossum's Universal Robots*	Arthur Miller
Colette	*Claudine's House*	Doris Lessing
F. Scott Fitzgerald	*The Popular Girl*	Helen Dunmore
F. Scott Fitzgerald	*The Rich Boy*	John Updike
E.M. Forster	*Arctic Summer*	Anita Desai
Graham Greene	*No Man's Land*	David Lodge
L.P. Hartley	*Simonetta Perkins*	Margaret Drabble
Jonas Jonasson	*The Hundred-Year-Old Man Who Climbed Out of the Window and Disappeared*	
Hans Keilson	*Comedy in a Minor Key*	
Anna Starobinets	*An Awkward Age*	

Poetry

Author	Title	Foreword writer
Geoffrey Chaucer	*The Merchant's Tale*	

NON-FICTION

Autobiography & Biography

Author	Title	Foreword writer
Melissa Valiska Gregory; Melisa Klimaszewski	*Brief Lives: Charles Dickens*	
Richard Canning	*Brief Lives: Oscar Wilde*	
Hazel Hutchison	*Brief Lives: Henry James*	
Fiona Stafford	*Brief Lives: Jane Austen*	

Food & drink

Author	Title	Foreword writer
Jerry Thomas	*How to Mix Drinks or The Bon Vivant's Companion*	

History

Author	Title	Foreword writer
Henry Mayhew	*Voices of Victorian London: In Sickness and in Health*	Jonathan Miller

Literary/Cultural studies & essays

Author	Title	Foreword writer
Charles Dickens	*On London*	
Sigmund Freud	*On cocaine*	
Ernest Hemingway	*On Paris*	
Harry Houdini	*On deception*	Derren Brown
Stendhal	*On love*	A.C. Grayling
Virginia Woolf	*On fiction*	
Leonardo da Vinci	*Prophecies*	Eraldo Affinati
Miriam Margolyes; Sonia Fraser	*Dickens' Women*	

Edgar Allan Poe	*Eureka*	Sir Patrick Moore
Rainer Maria Rilke; Maurice Betz	*Rilke in Paris*	
Jonathan Swift	*Directions to Servants*	Colm Tóibín
Daniel Tyler	*A Guide to Dickens' London*	
Virginia Woolf	*Hyde Park Gate News*	Hermione Lee
Virginia Woolf	*Carlyle's House and Other Sketches*	Doris Lessing

Travel writing

Author	*Title*	*Foreword writer*
Robert Byron	*Europe in the Looking Glass*	Jan Morris
F. Scott Fitzgerald	*The Cruise of the Rolling Junk*	Paul Theroux
Stefan Zweig	*Journeys*